Praise for *Technologies of the Self*

"Haris Durrani's wonderful tale is as much about family, jobs, friends and growing up as it is a[...] God—and that's as it should be[...] outlandish, it presages a great ca[...] gifts and a generous spirit."
—

D0396034

"Fantastic, taut, lyrical, funny, and vivid—a family history of faith, time travel, and selfhood in the face of saints and demons."
—Max Gladstone, author of *Last First Snow*

"Haris Durrani's debut is both a quirky coming-of-age story and a meditation on the technologies we use to make ourselves: immigration, religious conversion, science fiction, sex. It's so true to mixed experience, it feels defiant."
—Sofia Samatar, winner of the World Fantasy Award

"*Technologies of the Self* is brave and ruthless, gorgeous, and delicious. It is really magical and magically real: an unfiltered, unapologetic, and unforgettable narrative."
—Daniel José Older, author of *Shadowshaper* and the Bone Street Rumba series

"A subtle and controlled gaze at the contemporary coming-of-age that trusts the reader to travel across time and science. Prerequisites in demonology and philosophy not required but are recommended. This is the kind of yes-yes world-embracing storytelling to challenge plastic realism and announce a writer."
—Ali Eteraz, author of *Native Believer*

"Beautifully written, eloquent, Mr. Durrani's novella evokes time travel in the only way we can make sense of it—through memory. The book is thick with images that rise up larger than themselves, stronger than themselves, softer than themselves."
—Paul Park, author of *A Princess of Roumania*

"In the tradition of Junot Díaz, Durrani offers a rare peek into the rich, often surprising cultural complexities of being Latino and Muslim in post-9/11 America. An inimitable novella about wrestling with identity where the costs couldn't be higher. Funny, original, and wonderfully written, *Technologies of the Self* will keep you turning pages and leave you impressed."
—Murad Kalam, author of *Night Journey*

TECHNOLOGIES OF THE SELF

THE DRIFTLESS UNSOLICITED NOVELLA SERIES

Technologies of the Self   Haris A. Durrani

Faith Healer   Victoria G. Smith

TECHNOLOGIES OF THE SELF

— A NOVELLA BY —

Haris A. Durrani

The Driftless Unsolicited Novella Series

BRAIN MILL PRESS · GREEN BAY, WISCONSIN

Published in the United States by Brain Mill Press.

PRINT ISBN 978-1-942083-18-4
EPUB ISBN 978-1-942083-19-1
MOBI ISBN 978-1-942083-20-7
PDF ISBN 978-1-942083-21-4

Cover art © Mary Mazziotti.
Cover design by Ranita Haanen.
Interior design by Williams Writing, Editing & Design.

www.brainmillpress.com

Published by Brain Mill Press, the Driftless Unsolicited Novella Series publishes those novellas selected as winners of the Driftless Unsolicited Novella Contest each year.

For Uncle Tomás

CONTENTS

1. Leather   5

first memories   21

2. Iron   25

another memory   53

3. Flesh   55

the last memory   85

4. Fire   89

Credits   119

Author's Acknowledgments   121

About the Author   125

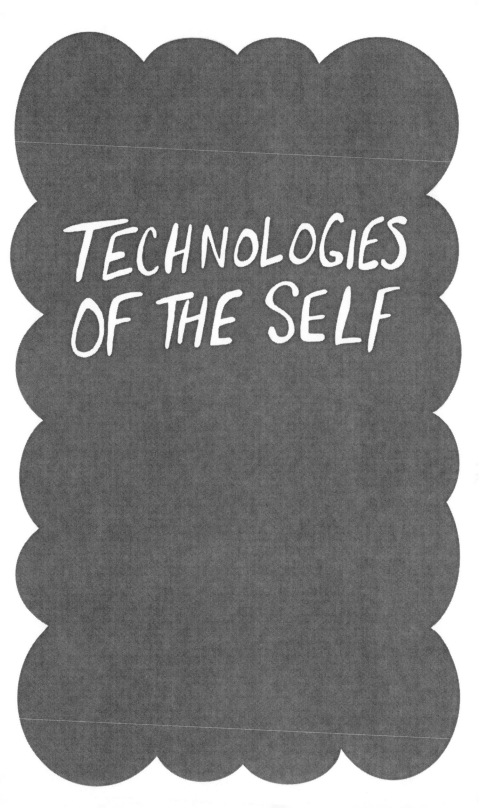

In such a morality, there is no reason to suppose there can ever be an end to the cycle of destruction, self-forgiveness, and the creation of new identities. When there are no obligations to the past, every destruction is only a new beginning, and new beginnings are all we can ever have.

—Talal Asad, *Genealogies of Religion*, on
Salman Rushdie's *The Satanic Verses*

✳

Mom tells me about the year Uncle Tomás became a man. It was 1967, she says, when her brother confronted three interlocutors and a being without definition. The first was their father, who whipped Tomás with his son's own leather belt in the musty kitchen of their Spanish Harlem apartment. The second was an older boy, who lodged a pickax in his chest for thirty-two cents of pocket change. The third was Veronica, the woman next door, who invited him in and displayed her parts. The last was Santiago, the insecure demon with a cosmic grudge, who pulled him through a door of no dimension.

"That was a bad year for Tomás," Mom tells me. "I think it's how he got so messed up. You should ask him about it. I don't know about the Devil though. Tomás says things."

When I ask my uncle, he grins and adjusts the pack of Marlboro Reds always tucked in his breast pocket. His eyebrows leap toward his prickly mat of gray hair.

"Oh, fuck! I remember that. Your mother is nuts, boy. Of course I met the Devil. I met him a bunch of times. You know I met the son of a bitch." He raises his fist in my face. "See this, boy? This is dy-na-mite. I fucked him up real good."

"But not the guy with the pickax?" I ask. We're in our kitchen eating Mom's sancocho. He's been complaining she makes too much soup, although he admits it's as good as their mother's.

"Hey boy, I'm here, right?" He gives me the finger and points below his cigarettes toward his heart. He leans forward, smelling of chicken, yucca, and ash. "Right there. I took it like a man. I'll tell you ... I'll tell you how it went down with all of them! How it really happened. You know something, boy?"

"I know." I roll my eyes.

"That's right. God loves me! I'm gonna fucking live forever. I ain't going nowhere. I wasn't back then, and I'm not going nowhere now."

Mom steps from the kitchen, ladle in hand.

"Tomás, man, you're old. You can't do those things anymore."

He turns to her and slurps his soup.

"Shit, Dolores." He waves a hand. "I'm gonna fucking live forever!"

1. LEATHER

✳

om carries her bowl to the dining room table, sits across from Uncle Tomás, and tells me about the time he slapped his teacher's ass. Mom was five. She and her siblings were playing baseball in the street outside their apartment building on 135th in Spanish Harlem when they spotted Tomás walking toward them in the distance.

"We gotta see this," Miguelito said.

"Papá is going to slap him as hard as he slapped Miss Feinstein," Carlos agreed.

Lourdes nodded. "C'mon. Let's go, let's go."

Gloria, the eldest at seventeen, was working in the Garment District.

Mom trailed after her older siblings through the front door, up all five flights, and into their apartment. There were no elevators. They rushed down the long hallway, weaving between clotheslines and hanging socks, and crowded into the brothers' room. They pressed their ears to the door and waited. Abuela had left, preoccupied by her son's deed, but Abuelo was waiting. They had glimpsed him in the kitchen leaning on the back of his faded white folding chair and lifting his plaid brown jacket from his shoulders with quivering fingers, as if he were suddenly an old man about to pee himself.

At last, they heard the door swing open. They giggled. "He's in so much trouble," Lourdes said with glee. "Tomás, man. Papá is gonna give him the whole treatment. You see. You wait and see."

"Shut up!" Miguelito whispered. "They're talking."

In our Connecticut dining room, Uncle Tomás sputters his lips. They are fuzzy with fine gray hair and wet with saliva and sancocho. "You weren't there, Dolores," he says. "You didn't see nothing. I'm the one who met the demon."

Mom shrugs and purses her lips the way she does when she knows she's won an argument—"Sure, Tomás."—but he's already turned to me, eyebrows jumping. He picks up where Mom left off.

In the apartment entrance, he kicked off his shoes and entered the hallway. The hall was narrow and dark, obscured by clothing that swung from long strings stretched overhead down the length of the corridor. At its end, the hallway broke right and then terminated with the children's bedrooms and bathroom. He knew his brothers and sisters were there beyond sight, ears pressed to the door, giggling. The hallway seemed to pulse. "I knew I was in deep shit," he tells me. "It was all quiet. Just car horns and people yelling on the street, you know? All quiet." He stopped where the open kitchen door met the hall, leaned against the outside of the frame, and held his breath.

"I can hear you," Abuelo beckoned. His Spanish was soft but insistent. He had performed this routine many times with his sons. They knew the rules.

Tomás stepped into the kitchen and avoided Abuelo's gaze. Light flowed from the window, illuminating the tile floor. It was freckled black with grit and oil.

"Stand in front of me."

Tomás shuffled until his toes were inches from Abuelo's polished black shoes.

"Remove your pants."

Tomás unbuckled his belt and undid his jeans. The belt buckle clattered onto the tiles as the rest slumped onto the floor. He stepped out of the pile, nudging it aside.

"Give me your belt."

Tomás knelt and slipped his belt from his jeans. He held it limply with upturned, trembling hands like the carcass of a half-strangled snake. He kept his nose upturned and his gaze on the window. The light there was bright and clear as rays of sun in water off the coast of La Romana. He missed his island. This place was cold, black, putrid, with too much noise and no rhythm. It would not shut up. Even now it was loud. Only its constant presence in his ears had rendered this moment silent, like a roaring surf heard in the confines of a shell. This city, I realize as he tells his story, is as restless and incessant as he was.

Abuelo snatched the belt from his hands and stared back at him. Tomás saw that he had brown eyes and flat lips that matched his own, the same big hands and big feet, the same desire to tell the other off. They shared a first name, Rafael. It was why people called Tomás by his middle name. One day he was going to fucking rule the world, ride through it and work schemes like Clint Eastwood's Blondie going town to town. Who cared what his father thought.

Abuelo held his tongue, I imagine, because this was his son, and he loved him. Tomás held his tongue out of rage.

Why grant his father the dignity of a response? He didn't deserve to be disciplined. He never deserved to be disciplined. He deserved respect.

Abuelo still wore his tie, but he'd undone his top button. He rotated his index finger in the shape of a cone.

"Turn," he said.

Tomás curled his lip but did as told. He stared through the open door and into the opposite wall of the corridor. The clothesline seemed to flicker as if one of his siblings had twanged it from the far end. He could smell habichuela in the air, and he could hear the plátanos still sizzling on the stove. If he concentrated, he could feel them sizzling, tiny reverberations in the fabric of this piece of the universe, as if he were very small and aware of the movement of every tiny thing.

"And now your briefs," Abuelo commanded.

Tomás blinked. He breathed for a moment before he tucked his thumbs under his sweaty white underwear and pushed it down to his ankles. His balls dangled dry and cold between his thighs. He heard the chair creak behind him as Abuelo rose.

"Bend over."

Tomás chewed the insides of his cheeks and focused on his toes atop the tiles. He inhaled the habichuela and plátanos. A moment passed, another, and with a grunt and a muffled whoosh, Abuelo struck him.

"Eyyaaaa!" Tomás screamed.

He heard Abuelo step back. "Do you know why this is happening, Tomás?"

Tomás balled his fists at his knees. He was going to be the king of the world.

"She was s-so hot!" he cried. "I c-couldn't help it!"

Abuelo's voice teetered to a higher volume. "Excuse me, Tomás?"

"She was s-so damn hot!"

He heard Abuelo step forward and swing. The pain came an instant later and burned.

"How dare you speak back to me!" Abuelo thundered. Again, he swung the leather.

"B-but she was s-so hot, Papá!"

Smack!

"B-but she was so fucking hot!"

Smack!

"Papá! I c-couldn't help it!"

Smack!

"Her ass was r-right there, what was I—"

Smack!

"Aaaa! Papá!"

Smack!

"Papá!"

The pain caught up with Tomás. It clung to him with urgency, singing shrilly in his ears. His back arched and his toes curled. His tongue twisted into itself and his teeth ground against one another. For a moment, he felt that he had left his body. First he believed he was in Abuelo's body, delivering his own wounds. And then the body of the light from the window behind him, old and waning as the day completed itself. And then he was in the clothesline, vibrating, pulsing, flickering to a rapid beat, jazz maybe, or bachata, but bereft of melody. All drums. He jerked his head as if from a pool of cold water and discovered himself in his own body again, neck craned upward, staring into the hall. He heard Abuelo's footsteps fade into an adjacent room. "Mi hijo…" Abuelo whispered.

Something black slipped from the clothesline. The tip of a boot, big as an ogre's, then a thick, armored pant leg sealed to the boot, followed by half a torso, an arm, the blade of a sword, and a morion with its visor lowered. The rest of the body fell through the clothesline, moving impossibly into three dimensions like a beam of light split along all trajectories. The figure knelt in the doorway, and at last Tomás could discern what it was. A knight in shining armor, suited in black and, kneeling, as tall as the doorframe. The figure reeked of gasoline.

The knight rested his forearm on his upright knee and with his free hand lifted his visor. It clanked. Beneath was a sheath of stained glass and a breathing apparatus. He punched a rusted protrusion beneath his chin. The apparatus exhaled and the glass slipped away, revealing blue eyes, bushy brown eyebrows, and thin lips adorned with a generous, vibrant red mustache. He made a point of smiling.

"Hello, Tomás. Didn't think I'd find you?" He spoke Spanish like a Spaniard, steady and formal, and at first Tomás did not understand his accent. The knight looked over Tomás's shoulder and shrugged. His garments banged and scraped against one another. He smirked. "Was her ass worth yours?"

"Who the hell a-are you, man?" Tomás demanded.

The knight paused and stroked his nose with an iron-gloved finger.

"What year is it?"

"Uh, 1967."

The knight spat onto the floor. "Shit." He shook his head. "Shit shit shit."

Tomás gestured with his chin at the knight. "You gotta problem?"

"I was supposed to kill you at a different time. Clean. No paradoxes." He stared off. "Shit. Shit shit shit."

"Kill me?" Tomás lifted a hand from his knee and beat his chest. "Why not k-kill me now, cabrón?"

"You would want to fight me. You stupid, stupid boy." The knight continued to stare into the wall. "But I can't. No paradoxes. I said that. No paradoxes."

"What did I d-do to you, man?" Tomás asked, digging a fingernail into his palm to counter the pain in his ass.

The knight tilted his head, but his eyes remained on the wall. The cupboards rose on either side of the door, bearing rows of plates, glasses, and condiments. The air was still, as if a hurricane had passed through these rooms hours ago. Tomás could hear his father's urine spool into the toilet in the adjacent room, and he wanted to call out. Fear and pain paralyzed him.

"You kill me. Killed me. Will kill me. One of those," the knight murmured. And then, with distant confidence: "It's a fucking mess." He faced Tomás and pointed his thumbs in opposite directions. "You and I, we're going along, downstream upstream. Time travel, man. How many times have we fought? Will we fight? Are we fighting? You're still here, you know, and so am I. I have to wipe the slate clean. I killed so many ... but you I can't. I try so hard. I really do."

"Hey! Answer me. Who the hell a-are you?" Tomás demanded, louder now.

The man shifted his left boot. His mustache twitched.

"You wouldn't remember. We're side by side, you and me." He began to turn. "I'll be back soon." He turned back. "Oh, and don't forget: Keep some change in your pocket. It's very important you do that, Tomás."

With this, the man turned. The floorboards groaned under his weight. He coughed, punched his chin, and slipped through the clothesline. The line twanged.

Tomás inhaled and shook his head. He found himself on all fours, drooling onto the cold tile. The belt lay behind him. The bathroom sink was on. He heard it gargle to a stop, and then his father stepped back into the kitchen.

"Do you understand now?" Abuelo demanded.

Tomás growled and rolled over; his underwear bound him at the ankles. He pulled it over his ass. Dominicans are blessed with big asses, men and women alike, but unfortunately for Tomás he had the flattest ass in the family. A white boy's ass. The pain was always sharper than it was for his brothers. It stung as he dragged his briefs to his waist.

He retrieved his jeans and struggled to his feet.

"Y-you will n-never understand me," he said, leaving the belt.

He wiped the slobber from his lips and stumbled into the hall.

"You're impossible, you know that, Tomás?" Abuelo called after him. "You are impossible."

Tomás shook his head and worked his way down the hall, leaning on the walls and groping for a handhold. He was numb now. He could only hear the drum of the clothesline. As he ambled toward his room, he stretched his hands above his head and looked up, running his fingers along the clothesline as if tracing the movement of constellations. But even without a roof, he knew the thick light of this city would obscure the night sky. In the DR, the universe sat easily on top of the world.

"That was the weirdest thing that ever happened to me," Uncle Tomás tells me.

By now, we've finished lunch, and Mom has ordered us to pull weeds in the backyard. Uncle Tomás is not good at gardening, but he works consistently. At least this is what Mom says. She pays him to do odd jobs around the house since he's unemployed and living off government disability checks. The rest of the family supports him too, although after he tried to smuggle Colombian heroin into JFK two years ago, they've begun to question their loyalty. "He's almost seventy," Mom told me once. "He can't be doing these things. He's a senior citizen." Uncle Tomás thrusts a clump of weeds into his trash bag and arcs his back.

"Weirdest thing," he echoes.

"A lot of weird stuff happens to you," I say. "Who was that guy? Are you sure you weren't hallucinating?"

Tomás emits a guttural laugh. "Boy, that was as real as you and me, that son of a bitch. That was the Devil."

"The Devil?"

"Yeah. Or, uh, *a* devil I think. The Devil's got all these guys under him and shit like that. Like bees or ants or, uh..." He trails off. "Yeah."

"Ah," I say.

He leans close to me, huffing cigarette breath into my face. "Oh yeah? I know his name. I-I can tell you what it is."

"Sure, Uncle Tomás."

"I can tell you," he promises, spittle flying from his lips. "He called himself... What was it?... Santiago. That mother was the realest fucking space knight I ever saw."

✳

We haul the bags of weeds and garden detritus to the garage, and Mom helps us drag them in. They are heavy and smell of pollen. I hold back a sneeze. She tells me about Uncle Mike. "He was always getting into trouble," she says. "He's such a crybaby, but he somehow got himself in all these situations."

When Miguelito refused to cut his Beatles hair, Mom tells me, Abuela waited for him to return from school before she ordered her other children to tackle him to the ground. Lourdes and Gloria pinned him at the wrists, Carlos and Tomás sat on his ankles, and Mom held him by the temples. Miguelito's mane flowed sweaty and thick over Mom's tiny fingers. She was the youngest. Abuela retrieved a large pair of scissors from the counter and knelt on the creaking wood floor, binding Miguelito's ribcage with the legs that had brought him into this world. She fitted his chin into the crook of her palm—"You listen to me, Miguel. You want the hair of a hippie? You can have it."—and, as he stared back in horror, she let go of his chin, clutched his hair, and sliced away unruly chunks. She left half his do untouched, wild, brown, and elbow-length, and reduced the other side to stubble, tufts protruding from his gray scalp like the skin of a poorly shaved dog. "There," she said. "Now you look like a real street monster. You like that?" His five other siblings, his cousins, and his friends ridiculed him. Two days later, he cut the rest himself.

The other siblings laughed, but they knew they too could become victims of their mother's wrath. They had evaded the Trujillato in the Dominican Republic, but a piece of it followed them. Today, we refer to the women of the Paoli family as the Paoli Generals after our ancestor General Pasquale Paoli. General Paoli freed Corsica from Italy and founded the world's first constitutional democracy. The Corsican Republic lasted little more than a decade before the French invaded, claimed the island for their own, and exiled

General Paoli to London. In time, he returned, universally adored by his countrymen, including a young Napoleon, as a symbol of justice and liberty, and he was elected into the French-subsumed government. When General Paoli sided with royalty in the French Revolution, Napoleon turned on him, and General Paoli, with the help of the British imperial fleet and the authority of King George III, chased Napoleon into France, freeing Corsica once again, this time from the French. But France quickly took back the island. General Paoli returned to London, where he lived his final days.

In the garage, Mom describes Abuela as the Paoli matriarch, an instrument of brutal reason. Outside in the grass, a squirrel raises its head, attentive to the sparse suburban traffic. A bird calls across the yard.

"They deserved it, you know," Mom says. "Our family has a problem with authority."

"Easy for you to say," Uncle Tomás interrupts. "She never beat you."

"That's because I was good," she says.

"It's because you were fuckin' spoiled!"

Mom rolls her eyes. When a child misbehaved, she explains to me, Abuela would wait for him or her to enter the shower. Usually it was Miguelito. After the water ran, she would unwind a metal coat hanger, open the bathroom door, rip aside the curtains, and swing at the shivering creature. He would squeeze his legs together, covering his privates. "I'm sorry!" he'd cry, and Abuela would swing harder. "Sorry isn't good enough!"

"That's what you tell me when I do something bad," I cut in.

"You're lucky I don't do the other stuff," Mom replies.

To his people, Pasquale was a general. But to the Italians,

the French, and later his royal friends in Britain—when revolutionaries in the Thirteen Colonies opened Paoli Taverns in his honor—he was a rabble-rouser. The Paolis were experienced in the art of discipline because they had played equal part punisher and punished, occupier and occupied, general and soldier. But more so the latter. Mom says we're kicked out of every place we go. My great-grandmother's ancestors migrated to the Dominican Republic from Germany. Pasquale ceded from Italy, then France, then was exiled for the second and last time to Britain. My great-great-grandfather left Italy for America, then America for the Dominican Republic as a U.S. soldier in the occupation in 1917, staying behind after the country claimed independence and losing his American citizenship after he spent years voting in his new homeland. Mom's family left the Dominican Republic to arrive here, whipping their tail from beneath the clamp of Ramfis Trujillo's boot as the U.S. invaded once again in 1965. I have to assume my time is coming.

✳

A week later we host a birthday party for one of my little cousins, Bella. Uncle Tomás isn't invited. Titi Gloria, Mom's eldest sibling, finds me sitting alone. I ask her about Trujillo, and she tells me about her relationship with the dictator's regime. Before they left the Dominican Republic, Gloria protested the Trujillato. Abuela told her to stay at home, but Gloria didn't listen. Abuela beat her harder and harder until one day she cracked open her daughter's skull.

Titi Gloria tells this to me with gusto, as if delivering one of her many sermons, when the family circles around a meal as she sings Jesus' praises while we grumble and rub our bellies. Titi Gloria's evangelical, gives grace with vibrato. Still, we ask her to give grace at every party, like this one, and she's careful about not calling Jesus "God." When she's done she asks Dad to come up and say something, and he'll refuse politely. Everyone will chime in, and he'll accept. Dad and Titi Gloria balance each other well. She had a hard time accepting Mom's conversion to Islam, but she's come to terms with it. Mom has told me the transition wasn't hard. She says she doesn't feel like she lost anything. Islam changed a few things, but a lot was the same. So were the families. Both were large, and both partied hard at weddings. She says she wishes Dad's family had been more dedicated to Islam, had been more willing to teach her values and practices that she would learn later. Dad and I are more Muslim now thanks to her. She's cooked ropa vieja and arroz con pollo with halal meat for the party, so I can still eat Dominican food. Her and Dad don't follow halal as strictly as I do, but they're happy that I do it.

While I dig into Mom's ropa vieja, Titi Gloria tells me what she thinks about Abuela's disciplinary methods.

"I was trying to do good in the world," Titi Gloria says, "but your grandmother was too afraid. You have to understand that we have to make sacrifices for the greater good. All it takes is one person. Look at Moses. Look at all the Prophets. Muhammad." She nods to me in acknowledgement. "They put their people before themselves. Dad was fine. But my mother was a hitting mother . . . No, I shouldn't say that . . . But if my mother went to hit Dolores, we'd all go in front of her. Otherwise Dolores was always hiding behind your abuela's skirts. Dolores, man . . . Your mom, she was spoiled."

"She was like an only child," I suggest.

"Yes! Like you. You are spoiled like your mother." She smiles and holds my hand.

I imagine Mom at nine years old walking home from school with her friends, wearing a little dress and white socks with black shoes the size of Christmas ornaments. She waits outside their apartment for Abuelo to arrive from work. He lifts her into his arms and holds her, his favorite child, and hands her a crisp dollar bill. "Buy some candy for you and your friends," he says. He always told her to share. Back then, Mom tells me a few minutes later as we watch Bella blow her candles, a dollar was enough to buy armfuls of sweets at the store down the block.

"Every day our father would bring her chocolate kisses," Titi Lourdes recalls begrudgingly, and from behind us Mom quips: "Yeah, and now I'm allergic!" As far back as I can remember, I've wondered vaguely about the origins of Mom's addiction to Hershey Kisses. It's her favorite candy. That and dark chocolate. She can still eat them, but her doctor says her body is beginning to react.

Every day after Mom shared her candy with her friends, Abuelo would buy her a new coloring book. She would fill it out in great detail, pressing her crayons hard against the lines but never crossing them. Tomás would watch, fascinated by the colors. He was a strange boy, incredibly handsome, blond, and tall as Abuelo. His sister's coloring amazed him. He was quick to take offense. He stuttered.

Last year, Mom showed me a yearbook picture of Tomás, and he looked nothing like the grizzled old man I know. His teeth were white, his face symmetrical, his hair short but full. Even in black and white I recognized that it was gold. Before he got arrested a few years ago, Tomás would walk around Washington Heights and buy those coloring books for adults, the ones with numbers associated with specific shades, from his friends selling cheap merchandise on the curb. He took the books to his apartment, the brothers' old room—which was his until Titi Lourdes refused to let him move back after his time in prison—lit a cigarette, and looked across the street at New York Presbyterian. He picked up his brush and painted. He would spend weeks on a project and, finally, produce a work of art. He's told me he's giving one to Mom for Christmas.

"Tomás?" Mom tells me after Bella's party, as we carry vacated, wet platters of watermelon to the kitchen. "When he got in trouble, he didn't give a shit. He talked back."

✳

Once Tomás had retreated to his room that fateful night in 1967, Mom tells me and Dad and Titi Lourdes over dinner that evening, Abuela returned, and Abuelo changed into his pajamas and ate with the rest of his family. After a quiet meal, Abuelo carried Dolores to his rocking chair, turned on the TV, and did what he would do every night until she graduated middle school. He reached down and cupped the heels of her right foot with the palm of one hand. With the other, he ran his fingers through the crannies between every toe. "Like this," Titi Lourdes recalls to me. She takes my hand and runs a finger between each of mine, one at a time. It's soothing. I have a vague sensation of Mom doing the same to me as a toddler, but I'm not sure if I've manufactured the memory. That night, Abuelo set down Dolores's right foot and picked up the left, performed the same ritual, and returned to the right. Eyes on the TV, he rocked back and forth, continuing like this until at last she slept.

first memories

Mom and Dad and I go out to the City a few weeks after Bella's birthday party. We catch an off-Broadway play and eat at a halal Turkish restaurant. We agree the Turkish food in New York is better than it is in Turkey, or at least Istanbul. It's summer, and the wind slides through the open window, raising our clothes from our sticky skin. Mom has my hand in hers. She squeezes it and reaches for Dad's.

"This is the sexiest thing about your dad," Mom says. "The back of his hand. I always thought it was the sexiest thing about him."

"Okay, Mom."

Dad laughs. "Not the only thing!"

"Of course," she says, looking at me.

The back of Dad's hand is broad and thickly veined. Tiny patches of dry skin cover the remains of old wounds.

I recall one of my earliest memories at our first home on the peninsula in Connecticut. I was four or five. I had perched on top of the living room couch, staring through the window across the street and onto the small dock. Beyond, the Long Island Sound rocked beneath the sunset. Dad sat beside me. I cupped my hands in front of me and prayed for fish. The next morning, I woke at dawn and ran to the window. The sky was gray, and the water beneath the dock boiled with striped bass kicking against the waves. Dad gathered the fishing gear. He helped me cast my first line and reel in my first bass. The creature was as big as me. He filleted the carcass and grilled it on the barbecue in the driveway. That evening I prayed again. The next morning, again, the water boiled under a gray sky. All I can remember is my excitement about the fish I caught. They were the largest wild animals I'd ever seen up close. I don't think I understood the idea of miracles.

When I was thirteen, Dad took me to Montauk. Since then we go every so often. He charters a boat and brings along family and friends. Last summer he brought Uncles Carlos and Mike. Uncle Tomás, of course, was not invited. We left the dock before dawn, and Uncle Carlos, the military vet, refused to chew raw ginger to stave off the seasickness. By noon his breakfast found its way out of him and over the stern. Uncle Mike brought his camera and documented the trip, preserving it in digital. Afterward, while we ate our catch on land, they asked me about girls. They told me I had a big fat Dominican ass. Dad chimed in—"And hairy like Pakistanis!"—and they laughed.

I rolled my eyes, but inside I knew. Yes, I said to myself with pride. Yes my butt is all of those things.

As long as I can remember, I always waited for Dad to arrive from work. I'd hide behind the door or under the stairwell or behind the curtains, and once he entered the bedroom I'd jump out and throw something at him, but he would know I was there. He'd whip out his belt and swing the leather at me. He'd chuck his dirty socks and blow his nose on tissues and toss them in my direction. We'd chase each other across the house until one of us became too excited and broke or almost broke something. Mom would blame Dad. "He started it," Dad would say, and she'd pinch him. "You encourage this behavior," she'd say. "He's a kid. You are an adult. You are a grown man!" But Mom does childish things too, like jumping into the pool with her clothes on or hiding chocolate in the freezer or eating too much popcorn at the movies. Uncle Tomás is the most obviously infantile adult I know, but there are fractions of him in each of us. Dad and I still mess around sometimes, even though I guess I'm also supposed to be a man by now. We end as we often did: in the prayer room rolling over the carpet, arms wrapped around legs, pulling each other's ears and noses and yanking out hair from any place on our bodies. We laugh so hard we slobber. Our history of wrestling is the reason I'm impervious to pain. We don't mind the hair, because we know it will grow back. It's in the family. My grandfather on Dad's side passed away with a full white mane.

But in the Turkish restaurant, Mom lets go of Dad's hand and tells me I must have my dad's mother's genes. She says I'm going bald. She says I better find a girl soon because in a few years I'll develop a bald spot and no one will marry me and her and Dad are getting old and don't I want my children to grow up with their grandparents around? Don't I want them to remember my mother and father?

"Do you want to end up like Tomás?" she dares. "Sitting on your ass all day and doing whatever? With no one?"

"I'm not going bald," I protest.

"Yes you are." With one finger, she scratches the top of my head in the place where Dad delivers nuggies. "Yes, you are."

2. IRON

✳

I learn many of the family stories this Christmas, but I've heard versions of them before. We're at Monica and Danny's home in New Jersey. Monica is my cousin, Titi Lourdes's daughter. My parents hate driving to Jersey because of the traffic, but we haven't seen everyone in a while. It's the first party Uncle Tomás has attended since the TSA caught him with five kilos of Colombian heroin at JFK. His parole officer is away for the holiday. "That bitch," he says to me. "She's always up in my ass." Dad and I are squeezed onto Monica's couch with all six Paoli siblings: Lourdes, Gloria, Carlos, Mike, Tomás, and Mom. I'm snacking on plátanos verdes.

My cousin Little Mike arrives from his night shift, bald, tattooed, and sporting an oversized white T-shirt. Mom always tells him to get rid of the tattoos. She says they're ugly. His wife, Marleny, and their two-year-old twins are already here. Little Mike is Uncle Mike's son from his first marriage to an Irish woman. Years ago, Mom used to make fun of Little Mike because he kept dating white girls. "No Dominicans?" she'd say. "You gotta marry a Dominican!" And he'd point to me—I was around ten years old—and say,

"At this rate I'll get married after he does." When he married Marleny a few years ago, I approached him and teased, "Hey, what happened?" He shrugged. "You took too long, man!"

Little Mike stretches over the coffee table toward Uncle Tomás.

"Felicidades, Tío," he exclaims. He takes Uncle Tomás's hand in his and makes his eyes bulge. "You still got that grip, man. You still got that grip."

"I'm not dead yet!"

"I can tell." Little Mike lets go, stands straight, and heads for the empanadas.

I want to try the empanadas, but Titi Gloria says they're chicken and beef. "Have them," she urges. "They're very good." After I decline twice, I tell her I've committed to eating halal. I've been eating halal since freshman year. Beforehand, I ate mostly organic, certified humane meats like Mom and Dad do. The halal industry is about as guilty of animal abuse as the rest of the meat market, and halal, as we see it, is more than calling God's name and slitting the jugular with a whetted blade. The ritual is about the moral treatment of animals. But we were loose with our progressive principle. When so many friends ate halal at college, I felt pressured to do the same. Three years later, I think it's a good thing it turned out this way.

"I eat halal now," I explain.

"Oh, that's okay," Titi Gloria replies. "That doesn't matter."

Dad overhears. "What do you mean, that doesn't matter?"

"You can eat whatever," Titi Gloria says. "It's not that important, at the end of the day."

"Do you know where your meat comes from, Gloria? Have you seen *Food, Inc.*? Do you know what halal is?"

"Come on, we all believe in God—"

"Gloria, you don't understand." He scoffs. "It's about a holistic respect for the animal. Do you know what shock treatment is? Sometimes the chickens are still alive when they cut them open. They feed them hormones and meat scraps and all kinds of shit…"

I know where this conversation is going. I leave and enter the living room, where I sit down with the rest of the family. Titi Gloria and Dad join us ten minutes later. On the couch, our fingers sprinkled with salt from the plátanos verdes, my aunts and uncles remember how Abuela used to make them. They are eager to recount the family history.

Titi Lourdes holds my hand and asks me if I remember Abuela.

"Yeah," I say and clench my jaw. I stare into the TV. A screensaver bounces a white tree through black static while it plays Christmas songs in Spanish. "I remember some stuff. I remember sitting in her lap." It's one of my earliest memories. We were in our Connecticut backyard for Abuela's seventieth birthday, and the family flocked around us for a group photograph. I was four years old. At home, Mom has it taped above the phone.

"You remember that?" Mom asks, surprised.

"A little bit."

I wonder if the memory is mine or if I've grafted it from the photograph, my personal history retrofitted like a replicant's from Philip K. Dick's *Do Androids Dream of Electric Sheep?* I have another memory of launching into Abuela's lap in the family's Washington Heights apartment. The memory is vague and full of light from the window above her shoulder, but I know it is real. Abuela was mountainous, with thick floppy arms and legs. Her lap was always soft and warm. I remember drawing pictures of her in the hospital when I was seven, but I don't quite remember what she looked like lying on the bed in New York Presbyterian. Mom hung my drawings on the hospital wall so Abuela could see them, and my aunts said these kept her alive another few days. Titi Gloria has told the story of Abuela's passing many times to me. Abuela whispered that she saw two angels hovering above her, beckoning her to follow. Titi Gloria sang hallelujah.

A week later, they buried her in Santo Domingo next to Abuelo, who I never met, and stored my drawings inside the grave. Uncle Mike cried the most. I've never seen anyone cry that much. His T-shirt was dark with tears. Tomás and Carlos dumped a bucket of water on him to cool him down. There was a lot of wailing. Muslims are not supposed to wail because it disturbs the soul, which remains in its corpse hovering alone in the darkness and the cold, waiting to be ferried to the afterlife. But I wailed so much that Dad had to carry me away. I didn't understand but cried anyway.

From the other side of the couch, Titi Gloria smiles at me. "You know I'm your grandmother now, right? You know that, right? I know you have your other grandmother still, but I am like your grandmother too."

"Yes," I say. She tells me this every time I see her.

I wonder how Abuela could do the things she did. My aunts and uncles speak of her with the same awe and love that I remember. Mom frequently complains to me about how nice Abuela was to Dad. Abuela always defended him, even when he was wrong. "And you know how Azra is," Mom has told me. "I had both your grandmothers to deal with!" Okra is a traditional dish in Pakistan, as it is in the DR. Abuela would cook Dad okra and lamb whenever he visited, although no one else liked okra and Mom thought lamb tasted gamey. Okra is Dad's favorite dish.

Still, Mom defends my abuelos despite their disciplinary methods. In fact, she says, they had every right to discipline their children the way they did. White people are too soft on their children.

"Did you hit *him*?" Titi Lourdes rebuts, pointing to me. "He turned out fine."

Mom points back at Titi Lourdes and the rest of her siblings. "I didn't need to! You guys were so stupid. You did stupid things. The only time I ever hit my son was when he ran away at the Bronx Zoo. Do you remember?" she asks me. "You were four or five. That was a stupid thing."

I remember hiding, but I don't remember Mom slapping me. The memory is filtered by haze, as if I'm staring through an opaque windowpane. I see bushes, grass, and something taller than I was. A bench or pillar. I crouched behind it, giggling but terrified.

"I thought I lost you," she says. "I was so scared."

These days she tells me stories about pedophiles, sex predators, and cannibals. "They have groups now," she rants. "Private clubs like AA. They sit around and they feel comfortable with these urges. And then they start thinking it's okay because they don't act on them, they're just urges. Like these two guys were in this online group for people who have cravings for eating people, and then they started hanging out together, and then one day one guy invited the other guy to his house and he killed him and ate him. All of him. No trace. I heard it on NPR. It's real."

"Mom," I say. "I'm twenty-one. No one's going to eat me."

She raises her nose. "Hey, you never know. You never know. These people are out there."

"Okay, Mom."

She returns to Abuelo. She tells me that doves and pigeons

would flock daily to the ledge of their apartment, and he would feed them bread and scraps from dinner. She said he was squeamish. The sight of blood threw him into shock. Whenever any of the children were badly cut, he would faint, and Abuela would have to take care of the bleeding child and her unconscious husband.

"So how could he whip Tomás?" I ask.

Lourdes shrugs. "I think it was a man thing. He did that routine with all the brothers. Mostly Miguelito and Tomás. Carlos was pretty well-behaved."

"Hey!" Uncle Mike teases. He's taking pictures of his twin grandchildren. He is into photography these days. He documents trips to lighthouses and boat rides on the Long Island Sound. He carries his hefty albums to share at family reunions.

"Fuck this," Tomás says, as if about to leave, but he doesn't.

Carlos smiles quietly.

"You did stupid things," Mom repeats. She pauses. "You should have seen how your grandfather talked to those guys on the phone when he got the call about Carlos's draft to Vietnam. He gave it to them. Never heard him swear so much. He never swore. He was always very polite but that time … man."

Beneath the Christmas tree, Little Mike's twins roll around and send tiny race cars over the lacquered wood. Uncle Mike lifts his camera from his chest and hunkers behind the lens. Uncle Carlos watches his granddaughter, Bella, jump across the room in her purple dress. She dances to music from the TV. The room fills with the smell of chicken and steaming beans. Mom is dressed in sparkling yellow and black, the kind of dress that often gets her mistaken for Pakistani, and Dad is wearing a long-sleeved button-down with a pocket over each breast like a guayabera, the kind of shirt that gets him mistaken for Dominican, a dark one with roots in Haiti. Dad presses a fist to his mouth and suppresses a belch, and my cousin Gregory, Uncle Carlos's son and Bella's father, raises his brow from where he's leaning on the doorframe and chuckles. "Nice one, Adnan."

Titi Lourdes finishes her empanada and purses her lips. Like Mom, she wants to remedy the image they've drawn of my abuelos.

"Your grandfather was a very honest man, very outgoing, a mind ahead of his time," Titi Lourdes assures me. "We came from an island where everyone was very behind of mind. They were not so progressive. He wanted us to be free."

Titi Gloria nods. "He told us, 'I want you to be your own person.'"

"Yeah," Mom says, "but that doesn't mean you go to protests and put your family in jeopardy. Who does that? If they caught you, you know what the Trujillato would have done to us? What they would have done to you?"

Dad laughs. "Yeah, Gloria, what were you thinking?"

"I was doing as the Prophets did."

"You think you were a Prophet?" Dad accuses.

She breathes. "No, I did *as* the Prophets did."

Uncle Tomás fidgets in his chair, lips sputtering, attempting to find his place in the conversation. He leans forward.

"I-I remember when I was working at the supermarket."

Everyone turns to him. He pauses, registering the sudden attention.

"Dad came by for subway money," he continues. "He had nothing on him. But I gave him everything I had in my pocket, fifty, sixty cents or something. 'I'll get the money,' I told him. 'Don't worry, I'll get it for you.' So I did. I gave him everything I had." He gesticulates with long, callused fingers. "I am always—always very proud of that."

He nods. He smiles and his face changes. The wrinkles evolve from carvings into hills, the scars from streaks to crescents. His teeth are yellow, and his eyes almost disappear beneath the tight folds of his thin lids. We stare at him for a polite moment before the conversation continues where it left off. *That's great, Tomás,* we want to say. *Cool story. Thanks for sharing. You blew our minds.* But we don't. That would be too insulting, wouldn't it? Would he even realize our sarcasm? Perhaps we don't care enough. I look at him and smile. He asks me about school. "It's okay," I say. I feel that I know him better than I do anyone else in the room. Maybe it's because I see him more than the others. He and Uncle Carlos help me move back into the dorm every year, and he works odd jobs at my parents' home in suburban Connecticut. My other aunts and uncles are offended that I haven't visited them in Manhattan since I arrived there for college a few years ago. I tell them I barely have time to hang out with friends. It's not a lie, but I wonder if subconsciously I don't want to see them. When I think about a good time to visit, I can't find one. There are too many things to do. It is hard being an engineering student. There isn't room to be much else.

Uncle Tomás and I listen as the rest of the family talks. We're both quiet, on the sidelines of conversation. He leans close.

"You got a girlfriend, boy?" He asks this every time we meet. He runs through his list of fetishes: "Italian? Chinese? Dominicans? Any Dominican girls? C'mon, what do you like?"

"I don't have a girlfriend," I reply. I still haven't told him that I did back in high school. A white girl who rowed crew, dirty blond with freckles and denim short-shorts. Her name was Glory. He would make fun of me. It's been almost four years, but I miss her sometimes. Every once in a while I think I recognize her in a crowd: on campus or the subway or downtown maybe. She is a fleeting image, the plain threads of her hair separated by breeze and her ears bare, emerging now and then from the anonymity of crowds like an apparition before returning into the sound of scuffling shoes and distant shouts and machines accelerating or decelerating from one place to another.

Uncle Tomás would laugh if I told him this. But she listened to what I had to say. Until Glory, I never felt that people heard me. I think she just liked listening. I don't think she cared what I actually said, but I didn't mind. Once during lunch we ditched the high school cafeteria to hang out in her car. She sat in the driver's seat and I sat shotgun, and she listened while I explained to her one of my many theories.

"I read this article recently in *New Scientist* about quantum foam. They were saying it's possible to view the universe as composed of an infinite quantity of mini black holes—MBHs—that are each infinitesimally small. Like the building blocks of reality. Not atoms. Black holes."

"That's cool," she said, taking my hand.

"Then I thought of this other article I read a while ago about loop quantum gravity. Part of it relates to the Big Bang, says that our universe is sitting in this giant black hole that's expanding and contracting like a heart." I raised my fist and clenched, then released. "The Big Bang was just one of a bunch of expansions, and the Big Crunch, if it happens, would be a contraction. Out and in, out and in. Goes on forever."

"What's that? The Big Crunch?" She blew hair from her face.

"Oh, it's like a reverse Big Bang thing," I explained. "The universe implodes. Anyways, so I was thinking: What if you combined these? Like, what if all the little black holes that make up the universe each contains a universe?"

"Whoa." She leaned over the shift, rested her head on my lap, and smiled at the roof of the car.

I stared into the red brick wall of the school's western facade. It was clean and bright.

"And then I thought, what if they're all the same universe? What if we're made up of these infinite fractal iterations of ourselves, like cosmic Russian dolls? Wouldn't that be crazy?"

"Yeah, it would." When I looked down, her eyes were closed. A moment passed before she opened them. "Can you kiss me now?"

"Uh," I said. I slipped my hands around the back of her head and shifted her away from my erection. "Yeah." I craned my spine and pressed my lips against hers.

"Your back okay?" she asked after a minute.

"It's fine," I lied. I looked up. This guy Rick and his friend were picking up books from his car. "It's Rick," I said.

She flinched and sat upright. He was looking at us, mouth open and eyes wide like we were doing a lot more than making out.

I would talk to Glory about this eventually. I'd tell her I didn't want to go very far physically. I'd tell her it wasn't in keeping with my faith. Looking back, since we were making out, I might as well have gone all the way. But she respected my request. At least this was what she told me. She was actually very considerate when I think about it. She'd ask whether we could kiss if she'd eaten bacon. She wouldn't drink at work socials, even though I didn't go to those parties. I didn't go to any parties. She wasn't a party girl anyway. "I know you wouldn't like it," she said. Uncle Tomás would have chuckled and shaken his head. "Be a man," he would have told me. "You either do what you're gonna do, or you don't."

✳

Once the conversation scatters, Uncle Tomás turns to me and continues his story. He tells me he recognized the Devil. "I woke up the next morning and my ass was stinging like wheeeow! And I thought, 'Hold it. I know that son of a bitch,'" he says. "But I wasn't sure. I had a—I had a hunch. You know. I had a hunch. Someone, uh—someone familiar. And then that weekend I saw him again." This was on a Sunday morning at Mass. The place throbbed with the movement of bodies and swayed with creaking benches. Gothic architecture rose above the crowd, intricate and vast as a beehive. As the church narrowed toward its front, the arches shifted from gray to gold. Bronze angels hung above the pulpit where Father Junior stood adorned in white and gold. The architecture seemed to unfold from its front, beaming light and sound direct from God. The church was chilly, and it smelled like a funeral home.

Tomás sat with his brothers and sisters. Abuela had placed Carlos between him and Miguelito, but that didn't stop them from reaching behind Carlos's shoulders to flick each other in the ear.

"Hey, you," Tomás jibed. "You got some shit in your ear."

"Hey, turkey," Miguelito shot back. "You, too."

Abuela overheard, squinted at the brothers, and pinched Tomás's shoulder. "Quiet," she hissed. "You are men, aren't you? Or are you boys?"

Tomás and Miguelito sneered and returned their hands to their laps. The congregation sang hallelujah, and Tomás closed his eyes and hummed. He thought about God and the Devil. He supposed the Devil had said to keep change on him for the purpose of giving his father the subway money. But why would that son of a bitch help him? The Devil was the Devil. The Devil did Devil things.

After Mass, my abuelos approached the lectern to ask the priest if he would consecrate a cousin's wedding vows in two months. Tomás waited with his brothers and shifted from foot to foot. As he kicked the steps leading to the pulpit's red-carpeted floor, his gaze wandered over the bronze statues. The angels hung precariously from beneath the golden arch, wings spread and javelins in hand. He imagined them in battle tearing the enemy limb from limb. But they were reserved, also. Their noses were upturned and their robes hardly wrinkled. As he describes this to me in broken sentences, I imagine that death for these angels was swift and simple, an act performed with efficient ceremony. On the wall beneath them, a larger-than-life Christ lay pinned to the cross. The Martyr stared into the empty pews with blank serenity, but his muscles writhed, and his hands and feet spilled trails of golden blood.

One of the statues was different from the others. It did not lean from the arch overhead, serene with hands outstretched. Nor did it stand pinned in anguish to the wall. The statue rose triumphant, brandishing a sword in the air. It stood beneath Christ as if to take the first communion. The statue seemed to soar above the back of a bronze horse that protruded from a rectangular cavern in the wall. The front hooves kicked into the air.

He had seen the statue many times in passing and thought

nothing of it. But the figure was undoubtedly that of Santiago the demon, the Devil, the knight, the spaceman, for it wore the same armor, the same morion, and the same Spanish sword.

Tomás read the plaque beneath.

SANTIAGO DE LOS CABALLEROS

Saint James of the Knights. Santiago, the patron saint of Spain. He was a household staple for many Dominicans. Standing there, Tomás recalled the image of Santiago in the homes of family in the DR and in apartments of friends in Manhattan. Santiago usually occupied miniatures hung beside the family cross, or else he sat above the fireplace, a gray sculpture the size of a fist.

At the party, Mom interrupts Uncle Tomás.

"Our mom wasn't into that stuff," she tells us. She says Abuela kept some Catholic relics, but not many. "We worship God," Abuela used to say. "Not stone, not iron."

✳

Uncle Tomás and I return to the couch, plates heavy with undivided piles of ropa vieja, habichuela, chicken, and mashed potatoes.

"So Santiago the Devil was Santiago the saint?" I clarify.

He nods. "Yeah, same guy."

"That's messed up."

I know that Santiago has many names. In Spain, he was Santiago Matamoros and Santiago Matajudíos, Saint James the Moor-Slayer and Saint James the Jew-Slayer. After Ferdinand and Isabella succeeded in their Reconquista and sent Columbus to the New World, he became Santiago Mataindios, Saint James the Indian-Slayer. Almost every Latin American country has named a major city after him. Missionaries transformed the Congo into a Christian state and inaugurated a national holiday in his honor, and when the Congolese were chained to ships and hauled to the New World, they celebrated the Feast of Saint James in the slave pits of Haiti, Puerto Rico, and the American South. Santiago, whatever he was, had travelled along the frontiers of the Spanish empire and even after its disappearance had lingered in the hearts of his disciples and their subjects until enough time had passed that the difference between child and parent was forgotten. He had ravaged the wombs of several peoples, discharged his seed, and slunk back into the folds from which he had come. He left peoples weak between the legs. His seeds had grown, born and reborn from each generation to the next, from occupation to occupation, and soon enough they revered the father who had made them.

Now Santiago had found a home in Spanish Harlem, ready to oversee the marriage of Tomás's cousin and hallow the congregation's prayers.

It's chilling. I swallow my food and rub the wetness from my eyes.

"So when you recognized Santiago, what did you do?" I ask Uncle Tomás.

He speaks through a mouthful of Mom's ropa vieja. "I didn't do nothing. What the fuck was I supposed to do?" But he did vow to keep his pockets empty. "No one tells me what to do," he says. "Not even a devil."

"But I thought the extra change helped my grandfather that day for the subway fare?"

"Fuck it!" he says. Bits of habichuela land on my lips. I

grimace and wipe them away. He smells of ash and chicken. "It was all a game, that bastard. I-I know it was. I do what I want to do. I'm your Uncle Tomás."

✳

After he graduated high school in spring of 1967, Uncle Tomás tells me, he observed his vow with dwindling focus. He struggled to manage without spare change, but he grew used to the walk from 135th to the supermarket and back. His boss didn't let him run the cash register or oversee the employees, God forbid, but they needed someone to move products from delivery trucks into storage and from storage to shelves. Mostly he hauled carts of bottled water and milk through the back and carried heaps of meat from the butcher's shop and heavy fruits like watermelons and cantaloupes. Sometimes his boss asked him to move products from aisle to aisle, but he often misplaced them, confusing ice cream with yogurt and hot sauce with salsa.

The storage room was gray and dark, and as his cart rolled and clattered across the cement floor, Tomás would often hear the sound of heavy metal. At first he mistook these noises for distant percussion—a band playing on the other side of the wall—but they seemed to escalate week by week. They were chaotic and bereft of pattern. Maybe, he thought, it was a music he did not know. He tried to locate the sound, but it seemed to come from every direction. After a month, it was loud enough that he recognized it as the sound of the demon's clanking armor. The demon was there. He lurked inside the edges of everything. Every straight line in the room blinked at him like winking static when he pulled the plug on his old TV in Santo Domingo. The edges along the enormous freezer's doorframe, the storage room door, the cart, the sharp hem of his jeans. The demon lived in the pulsing corners of the room as he had lived in the clothesline, making noise as he moved around Tomás. When Tomás was alone in the storage room, he'd lean into the nearest corner, smelling oil and rat piss. He'd lean so close he dabbed his nose with grit, and he'd declare his intentions. "I don't kn-now what you want from me, but I'm gonna find you. I kn-now what you look like, man. And I kn-now where you are."

Of course, Santiago was everywhere. He was on his friends' personal altars, he hung from their walls, and he rode his stallion through the front of the church every Sunday. These words were meaningless, but Tomás said them anyway.

He considered telling someone, but he knew his parents would scold him. "Tomás," his mother would say, "what is wrong with you?" His father would shake his head. "You need to take things seriously, Tomás." And his siblings and friends would make fun of him. "Tomás has an imaginary friend! Tomás is going crazy! Tomás is certified insane! Tomás is so stupid!" His boss would fire him. "I knew you were a retard."

One day on his walk home from the supermarket, a group of older boys cornered him in an alley. It had rained a few days before, and the sky was particularly clear. He imagined he was walking along the bottom of the Caribbean and that sunlight arrived here as it did in the sea, as pillars of white. Ambiguous, ubiquitous, and clean. The sidewalk was so bright he forgot the stains of gum and ash and imagined it was sand, pure and soft between his toes as it was in the Dominican Republic. The skyscrapers were buoys and boats and the ruins of Taíno architecture and conquistador monuments. They rose above him, old and new, barnacled and sleek, blurry and inconsistent as seen from below. The air was the perfect temperature, crisp but warm, and if he pinched his nose he could shut out the stench of Manhattan and pretend he was holding his breath. He was good at holding his breath. He was the best swimmer in the family, and the Paolis were a family of swimmers.

As he moved through the urban waters, he heard the sound of loose change. He slipped a hand into his pocket and realized he had deposited a quarter, a nickel, and two pennies there to be spent later on candy at the dollar store. Unlike Dolores, he had to buy his own fucking candy. But he didn't think much of it. It had been a while since the demon paid him a visit. He slipped his fingers out of his pocket, and a moment later the telephone line overhead vibrated. He continued walking, ignoring the escalating noise.

Seconds later the line burst into discordant song. It played notes out of key but with strange consistency, like a recording heard in reverse.

Told you so, a voice whispered in his ear, so close he mistook it for his own.

Behind him, four boys closed in. "These big black kids," he says to me. "They start following me down the street. They heard the change in my pocket and the biggest guy, he goes—"

"Hey you, whatchyou got in there?"

Tomás turned. A scowl distorted the eldest boy's baby face and revealed pearl-white teeth cracked along the edges. He was wearing jeans and a handknit sweater the color of pasteles.

"I d-don't know," Tomás replied. "What do you care?"

"I'm a little short. Could you spot me some change?"

The boy stepped forward, and his posse followed. Tomás

could smell hard liquor and sweat. The city returned to itself then, penetrating his memory of the DR with tendrils of soot. He noticed the gum and the cigarette butts on the sidewalk, heard the traffic and the thunder of planes overhead, tasted iron on the tip of his tongue.

Tomás licked his lips.

"No way. I-I earned this."

The boys circled him, and Tomás, stammering, stepped backward.

He found himself in the mouth of an alleyway. Fire escapes crisscrossed above him as if he were floating beneath a fleet of sinking ships at anchor, chains leading haphazardly toward the surface. The boy with the baby face reached into the small of his back and drew a pickax from a belt loop. The tool was the length of the boy's forearm, wooden and smooth along the handle and dark gray along its iron head. He swung it into and out of the alley shadows. Sunlight sparkled along its edges and gathered at its sharpest end.

The boys surrounded him. One stiff-armed Tomás into the wall. Tomás's ass met brick, and his change jangled in his pocket.

Tomás pushed back and raised his chin. The boys moved closer. They shook and howled and shouted at him as if in trance. Tomás growled back, one with God, alive with the rest of Creation. *I am the Truth,* he thought. *I am the end of the line. Don't fuck with me.* But they were not his words, were they? They were another's also.

The knight climbed from the fire escape, sliding out of the places where the black metal shone brightest. He stood, neck bowed beneath the fire escape, gargantuan and incongruous. The suit had abraded itself in places where it was intended to slide side by side like bulky scales. As the demon adjusted, his suit groaned with the reverberations of tectonic movements. Above, the power lines hummed. The telephone poles began to spin. The dumpsters rattled.

"Don't fuck with me," Tomás said to the boys.

"Excuse me?" the baby-faced one replied. With his free hand, he held Tomás by the lapels.

"You kn-know what I said." Tomás raised his fist.

"Tongue tied, eh?"

"Retard!" another jeered.

Tomás spat into the boy's face and struck him across the jaw. The boy laughed, let go of Tomás's shirt, and stepped back. His friends drew tighter. Tomás struck into flesh and leather as he drowned in sweat and thick cheap cologne. He heard a shout, and the boys scattered. The baby-faced one stepped forward, pickax drawn. "About that dough."

He whirled the handle once, twice, and allowed gravity its course. Tomás heard static, shivered as a gust flowed over the crown of his shoulders, and, with searing heat, the iron pierced his chest. The pain ignited in his heart and burned. Later, he would remember the soft complaint of torn flesh and the sound of crunching bone like concón ground between molars. For now he could feel nothing except the hot metal nuzzled between his ribs. It was suddenly very cold and wet. For a moment he glimpsed the boys standing over him, felt them riffle through his pockets. "Fucking pennies, what he fight for this shit for?" they muttered. He smelled Santiago's breath, ashy but mixed with disinfectant, and glared as the demon rose from the shadow of the fire escape and parted the boys, who meandered away as if anticipating his movement. Now erect, Santiago's height extended past the first story of the fire escape. "What he fight for this shit for?" the boys kept saying, tossing the coins from palm to palm as if the Devil were as banal as the sidewalk beneath their feet. Santiago moved toward Tomás. With each step, the dumpsters shook like cages. Tomás lay against the wall, arms weak, lids drooping, prodding the wooden handle of the pickax. The demon stretched toward Tomás, fingers splayed the width of a coconut palm's spread of leaves, and drew the pickax gingerly from his chest. Tomás screamed and shivered. "Told you so," the demon whispered. "I told you I was going to kill you." He smiled, nodded once, and called after the boys: "You forgot something." The boy turned, grimaced, strode to the toe of the demon's right boot, and craned his neck. "So I did," the boy said. The demon wiped the pickax through his mustache, laying streaks of crimson, and tossed it at the boy's feet. It danced briefly on the ce-ment. "On your way now," the demon murmured. The boy hooked it into his belt. "Appreciate it, sir," he replied, and followed his friends down the block. With feet still pointed away from Tomás, the demon twisted and grinned. The suit groaned, and the fire escape clamored, restless and impatient.

The moment passed. The demon slipped into the old yellow evening light. The light slipped into the shadow of the fire escape.

"Didn't tell me nothing," Tomás hissed into the shadows. "I'm gonna kill *you*."

His head throbbed and his body grew colder. He bit his tongue to distract himself from the pain. His tongue tingled with taste of blood. He wedged his behind into the wall and sat straight. Moaning, he arched his neck toward the pink sky, visible through the cross-sections of black metal. Hot, thick fluid poured from his chest and pooled at his thighs.

"I'm not gonna die. I'm not gonna fucking die. I'm—I'm g-gonna live forever."

Tomás raised his right hand and flexed his fingers. He considered them with mild disgust before he clenched his teeth and shoved his index through the ripped cloth and flesh. His body embraced the finger and molded to fit its shape. Inside, he felt damp and warm. He slid up against the brick wall and stumbled into the street. New York Presbyterian was eight blocks away.

He hobbled down the sidewalk, head held high, jaw taut, finger wedged into the cavity in his chest. Pedestrians stared at him and kept their distance. Several moved to the opposite side of the road. Mothers held their children against their legs. "You see that?" a woman said to her son. "That's what happens when you don't behave." Tomás snarled, but he couldn't speak. He was terrified of blacking out. The woman grunted and wrapped a hand around her son's shoulders.

As he approached the hospital, Tomás felt his body temperature rise. He checked into the emergency room and sat down. He looked absently at the finger in his chest. The lights were bright and white. His arm began to cramp, and the pain escalated. He rocked side to side. He heard groaning metal in the lightbulbs, and for a moment he thought he glimpsed the demon's boot swing from the ceiling.

After several minutes, he approached the desk.

"Hey," he said, "I got a hole in me. I n-need to see a doctor." He wiggled the finger in his chest.

The secretary looked up. "What's your name?"

"Rafael Tomás Paoli."

She looked down. "It will be half an hour."

Tomás shook his head and leaned closer. "You l-listen to me. I'm in pain. I need to see a doctor *now*. You hear me?"

The secretary winced. "I'm sorry. You have to wait your turn." She gestured at the sparse crowd in the ER. "They have to wait, you have to wait."

Tomás swore. "That's it that's it that's it!" He stumbled closer to the countertop and wiggled his finger again. "See this? Do you see it?"

The secretary made a point of frowning. "Yes I do, Rafael."

"Tomás."

"Yes I do, Tomás."

"Fuck it," he exclaimed. "Here you go!" He yanked his finger away with the poise of a wild conductor, perhaps at his great-great-uncle's opera, and blood squirted onto the counter and the secretary's desk.

"Vooosh!" Uncle Tomás tells me at the party. "Blood everywhere. Everywhere!"

The secretary screamed and bolted from her chair, hands raised as if he were robbing her at gunpoint.

"Fine! Fine!" she said. "The doctor will see you."

Uncle Tomás pinches me and laughs. "You shoulda seen her face, boy. Turned out the pickax missed my heart by thiiiiiiis much." He gestures with index finger and thumb. "Just a hair!"

After the doctor stitched his chest and he was alone, a metal finger parted the hospital curtains and the demon entered. Now he was only ten feet tall.

"By a hair," the space knight whispered. "I was so close, wasn't I? God thinks It is so funny. It thinks this is not an equal battle. It thinks I am a pawn. I'll show God funny." He continued to mutter to himself as he slunk off, suit barking metal on metal, but he stopped for a moment. "Anyways," he called over his shoulder, quietly and with remorse, "I'll see you at the neighbor's place."

✳

Uncle Tomás is still eating habichuela and plátanos after we've moved on to dessert. He is the slowest eater in the family. He piles his plate high, but he stays thin. Mom says it's because of how he eats. "We should eat more like Tomás," she says. "Digest our food properly." It's one of those things Uncle Tomás does better than we do. It's a special thing. I don't think he realizes it. Food is not very important to him. "I tell you boy, that Devil was real," he says. "God loves me. God fucking loves me. No demon can put an end to me." Mom points at him with her fork. "You're very lucky, Tomás," she counters. "And all for a few pennies!"

"Ah, shit, Dolores." Tomás waves a hand at her as if swatting insects. Balancing his pile of food in his right hand, he curls his left into a fist and beats his chest. "I'm here, right? I made it. Those older kids thought they got me, the Devil thought he got me, but no one's got me. Me and God, we got a thing going on. The Devil? He planted the change in my pocket. He had a whole other thing going on, you know, with those guys and the pickax. To hell with the Devil, boy. I'm not going nowhere. We're not even on the same playing field. I killed him, didn't I?"

"If you killed him, why's he still alive?"

Tomás looks at me. "You never seen *Terminator*, boy?"

I nod. I can go with that. "Well," I say. "When did you kill him?"

"Patience, boy. I'm getting there. Anyways, why else would he act like that? Like I already fucked him over?"

I laugh. "Because he's the Devil."

Tomás raises his eyebrows. "Not like this, boy. Him and

me, we go way back. So back I don't even know. You'll see. I'll show you how far back we go."

Dad lifts his plate toward us. "If I met the Devil, I wouldn't run. I'd have so many questions, you know? I'd want to talk to him, figure out how he's so messed up. I'd ask him about Hitler. And I'd fight him. I'd give it to him. I'm not afraid of the Devil."

"That's what you say," Mom says, rolling her eyes.

"That's right it's what I say."

Mom looks me in the eye. "You know what your abuela used to say? She used to always stay away from this kind of stuff. You don't go near it, okay?"

"Okay," I say.

She tells me, as she has many times, that if I'm on the sidewalk and I think someone's following me, I should limp and flail and act like a crazy person. She says that when I'm on the subway, I should sit next to black people, especially black women or big black men coming from a blue-collar job. "White guys in suits are the first ones to run. The one time I trusted a white man, that was the closest I ever got to getting raped," she tells me. Her favorite movie is *The Matrix* because the antagonist is Agent Smith, a well-spoken white man in a business suit. "That's how the Devil really looks," she says. "He doesn't look like a bad guy. He wears a suit and a tie, and he's very polite."

✳

After I finish Uncle Jimmy's golden flan, Marcos tugs my wrist and asks me to play. He's been asking me all night, but I kept telling him I was eating, which I was. I also wanted to hear the family stories, even though my older cousins have tried to bail me out several times. "Hey, can you help me with this?" they'd say, interrupting the conversation, and once I got there they'd lean in: "Those old farts not boring you, are they?"

Marcos drags me upstairs, my thumb gripped in his fist. He is Monica's son. He was born in Santo Domingo with prune belly, shaken up inside like he'd fallen off the wrong end of a teleporter. The doctors said he had days to live. Only an American hospital could fix him. Titi Gloria rushed Monica and Marcos to the airport. They would have missed their flight if Titi Gloria had not begged and pleaded and cried on her knees until the flight attendants opened the gate and let her through as she screamed hallelujah with her arms in the air. In Manhattan, she arranged for her colleagues at New York Presbyterian to operate on Marcos. They, too, suspected he would not survive the week.

Ten years later, he is dragging me to his room on Christmas. I hear stories about him in school. He's quite the ladies' man. He reminds me of what Tomás must have been like when he was this age. Smart-mouthed but always smiling, misbehaving but loving and well-loved. Determinedly macho. In every generation of the Paoli family, at least one of us comes into this world out of order. Tomás was born with meningitis, Uncle Mike and I with abnormally small right ears. Mom says it's a blessing. It's how Uncle Mike got out of Vietnam.

In Marcos's room, his sisters Emma and Sophia point at my ear.

"Why is your ear so small?" Sophia asks.

"Because I'm a mutant." I grin. "I'm like an X-Man."

"What?"

"I'm like an X-Man."

Marcos groans. "Go away, we're playing now! No girls!"

"Be nice to your sisters."

"Uh-huh."

Their friends pile into the room as Marcos boots his Xbox.

"Let's see," I say, "what are we playing? What d'you have?"

Marcos sneers at the girls and hands me a controller. His is camo green. The flatscreen erupts with noise. He tosses a few cases at me.

"I got everything," he says. "I got *Call of Duty.* I got *Resident Evil.* I got *Mortal Kombat.* Whatever."

I frown. I'm not a video game person.

"Marcos, these are violent games. You don't have like *Need for Speed* or something?"

He glances around. "No."

"Well, I don't like to kill people. It's mean." I consider my options and decide on what I suppose is the least bloody. I can still see red spewing from Uncle Tomás's chest. "Let's do *Mortal Kombat,* okay?"

"Okay."

Marcos pops in the disk and sets up our game, but his sisters and their friends burst into laughter. "C'mon," he says to them and jumps from his bed, pushing them out of the door. They scream, and Monica storms in. Marcos is quiet.

"Marcos?" she shouts. "What are you doing? Come here now. Now. Did you hear me, Marcos?" She looks at me, eyes wide and palms open. "Sorry about this."

I smile as she pulls him from the room. "No problem."

"I didn't do anything!" he yells. "It was them!" And then to me, with sudden, quiet conviction: "Don't worry, I'll be back."

I shrug and sit on the bed. He had started the match. Bella sits down next to me and begins to play. She sends her character kicking into empty space. I stare absently at mine, a tall, dapper man with a mustache and sword, and fiddle with the controls. I scroll through the options and select armor. Thick plates of metal swarm around his body and assemble into a coherent shape. He is taller now. The metal is black and shining. I toggle the joystick, and the speakers tremble as my character steps forward. The stand vibrates in a state of ecstasy. I let go. Without prompting, the figure turns, plunges his thin blade into the earth, and kneels. He peers out of the screen and searches until his eyes meet mine.

another memory

In high school, our robotics team toiled late nights in the basement. We spent hours working, and if we didn't like what we'd built, we'd take the machine apart and do it over again. Mom would freak out. "What are you doing?" she'd exclaim. "Don't do that! Now you have nothing! What you had was fine." Dad would laugh. "Let them be," he'd say. Mom would make us clean up every month or two because we'd scatter parts and scrap metal across the ground. When we had to cut zip ties as part of our robot's sweeper assembly, we littered the floor with sharp bits of plastic like shavings of coal. At some point that night, I leaned back, palm against the tile, and drove a shard of black zip tie into my wrist.

There was no pain at first but lots of blood. The tiny wound ached as I raised my arm and discovered red pooled in the creases of my hand. I remembered that Dad said he knew how to read hands, that he had memorized palm-reader tricks in high school when he ran his own lawn mower business to support his four siblings and parents.

My buddies, busy with the robot, didn't notice as I walked upstairs and ran water over the wound. The blood kept flowing, and I felt numb. I stumbled to the dining room table and collapsed onto a chair. I told Mom and Dad I was dizzy. Dad held my wrist and said, "Oh, Jihad, that's a very serious place to hurt yourself," and I blacked out.

I woke up a few moments later. Mom was scolding Dad. "You shouldn't've scared him like that," she was saying as he closed my fingers over a root beer.

"You need sugar," he ordered. "For the blood pressure."

Someone had tied a kitchen rag around my wrist. An ambulance arrived, and an officer walked in. He saw the bottle, label facing away from him, gaped at my slit wrist, and was about to suggest I'd attempted suicide before Dad chuckled and turned the bottle.

"It's root beer," he assured the officer.

Mom shook her head.

"He's just like his grandfather," she said to the officer. "Couldn't stand the sight of blood."

3. FLESH

*

After winter break, I meet my friend Kareem for lunch. He works in the fabrication lab. I take the stairs to the basement of the engineering school and pull open the door. It's hot and stuffy. The laser cutter is wedged into a makeshift wooden shack in the far corner, and four glass walls cordon off diagonally opposite quarters of the lab. Inside the glass enclosure in front of me, three guys hunch over a lathe. Another slides a beam through a jigsaw. The lathe sings, and the saw roars intermittently. I stick my head through the office door. Kareem is out, but Manny is at his desk. Manny is the manager, and he's the coolest guy in the lab. He's thin and balding, but he moves with the energy and agility of a middle-aged Peter Parker. I remember when he helped our research group mill a part for our robotic arm my freshman year. He spun the drill into a high-pitched blur, leaned over the mill, and played with the dials like a DJ. Milky coolant splashed over the laser-cut wood. "That's the magic, man!" he shouted, nodding to an unheard beat. "Woooh! Look at that. That's the magic, man. That's the magic."

I lean against the doorframe. "Hey," I say. "Kareem around?"

Manny looks up. "Hey, man. What's up? Yeah, he's around. I think he went upstairs."

"Cool."

"You're graduating, right?" he asks. I'd always meant to work at the lab. They mentor a robotics team in Harlem for a tournament I'd competed in during high school. I miss the excitement of those tournaments.

"Yeah. It's my last semester."

"Whew. Time flies."

"It does." I laugh.

"Where you heading next?"

"I dunno. Something related to technology, law, and, uh, policy." No robots.

He raises his eyebrows. "That's a mouthful. I'm sure you're going to go on to do great things."

"I hope so."

"No, I'm sure of it." He smiles. "You always were."

I nod thanks and wait outside the office. The lab coughs and clanks, and I begin to sweat underneath my jacket. I slip the gloves from my hands. A warped plate of black metal seesaws on the table in front of me. The plate is scablike and bulky, like a piece of Santiago's suit. I'm pretty sure that's what it is. I've been trying not to think about what I saw in Marcos's video game. I shiver and eye the laser cutter shack in the corner. Manny has painted it white and hung strips of plastic from the opening to prevent a fire hazard. I remember when Kareem met our research team three years ago and taught us how to use the machine. He got excited when he figured out I was Muslim and more excited when I told him Mom was from the Dominican Republic.

"Oh, dude!" he exclaimed. "Dude. You dating any Dominicans?"

"Not really?"

He punched me in the arm. "Latina chicks are so hot, dude. You gotta hit that up. You got access, you know? I'm Egyptian. It's here and there with us. Same with Pakistanis. Asi asi." He winked. "But dude. Dominicans, man. You got access. You gotta key that in. The Dominican side. Oh, man. Oh, dude."

"Uh, sure."

I spent a year assembling in the robotics lab in the building next door and machining parts in the basement of the engineering school. Most of this time was spent with Kareem, who was meticulous in his preparation of each part. He blasted the Rolling Stones, Led Zeppelin, Billy Joel, Red Hot Chili Peppers, and Quentin Tarantino soundtracks through the lab speakers, unearthing vivid childhood memories of Dad playing music on long drives to Vermont. Kareem liked that I was president of the Muslim Students Association. He had graduated a few years before me and had worked on the MSA Board when he was an undergrad. We discovered we ran in the same friend circles with young alumni. ("You know Omar?" "Yeah." "You know Rayan?" "Yeah." "You know Shan?" "Yeah." "You know Hajira?" "Yeah.") He lingered on the edges of my social field of view, here in the basement lab where it was hot and loud, hidden under the Greek pillars and Roman numerals and offices and suits and libraries. Here beneath the foundation, where it clanked like rusty clockwork and reeked of gasoline, sawdust, and burning plastic. Here where Santiago got his parts.

"Don't tell anyone on the MSA I'm here," he cautioned. "My parents are trying to hook me up with a family friend around campus and word spreads and I already got this girl, you feel?"

"Sure, man," I agreed.

He explained his evolution to me while lathing a shaft for our robot's wrist.

"I got disillusioned like every Muslim gets in undergrad, and I was like, 'Fuck it.' It's too much dealing with these people, you know? But you're president, man. That's very cool. You're not like the rest of those idiots." He looked up. "Don't be like me. I want to make sure you don't end up like me. I got fucked up. Don't let that happen, man."

I shrugged. "They're not all idiots. There are some really good people doing good work, I think. Smart and faithful and dedicated."

"Yeah yeah yeah. I know what you're saying." He removed his goggles. "But you know what I mean. You get it."

I avoided Kareem's gaze.

"Yeah, I do," I conceded. I missed the easy camaraderie of my high school robotics team, when the five of us relished the long, torturous hours. If the specter of NYPD surveillance and the university administration's complicity in it wasn't burden enough for Muslims on campus, we had our own differences to contend with, too.

He returned to the lathe and told me about his plans. He wanted to save enough to purchase or build his own boat, and then he would buy a shitload of supplies and take a copy of the Qur'an and maybe some Hadith and maybe some Al-Ghazali—but mostly just the Qur'an—and he'd sail the world. "I wanna get away from all this shit. I want it to be me and God, one on one."

I laughed a little bit and thought about Titi Gloria and

Uncle Jimmy, who used to sail to and from Puerto Rico and Manhattan.

"That's cool, man," I said, "but you know Muhammad, peace be upon him—he came down from the mountain. He didn't sit there in his cave meditating on Gabriel's message. He descended. Islam is about the people too. It's about this world."

I felt like a hypocrite. I prefer the cave on the mountain, too.

"I know," Kareem replied, "but I need this. I need to, you know, sail the world."

I smiled. "Like Sam Jackson in *Pulp Fiction*."

He pointed at me and yelped with joy. "Yes. Like that. That's fucking it. We vibe, dude. We so vibe."

Now, two years later and thirty feet away from the spot where he'd lathed the robot's wrist, Kareem finally arrives at the lab. I don my gloves. He takes my hand and we chest-bump. "Salaams dude," he says. "Gimme a sec." He drops off a few parts and grabs his jacket. "I'm so glad we finally get to have lunch. It's been a while. Sorry for my rants." He has a habit of sending me long emails about the state of the ummah or Shari'a or the latest radical nutjob. I don't mind, but I'm always too busy to read and think about them deeply. I tell him this. I tell him I prefer talking in person. It's more valuable, I say. But I know I do the same to my other friends.

We walk down toward the nearest halal dive on 125th and Amsterdam. We miss it at first and double back and miss it again. When we walk in, we see the place is changed. The once-open kitchen on the right is now barely visible behind the cash register, which has moved to the back. The shelves are higher, and somehow they don't seem to hold as many hookah.

"Whoa, it's totally different," I tell the waiter.

"Yes," he says, smiling.

"It's been a while," I explain.

Kareem and I sit down and order shawarma. We talk about how hard it is to work as engineers. We're implicated in military and economic power. We talk about the bureaucratization of the aerospace industry. The general public has little say in what is supposed to serve as a project for the good of humanity. I tell him about Boeing's X-37 orbital drone, an autonomous space shuttle whose details remain classified. I tell him premodern understandings of Shari'a might provide legal structures that favor plurality and community empowerment over centralized power. Kareem nods and raises his hands in delight. It's like I'm ranting to Glory, but Kareem isn't just willing to listen. He understands. He says 3-D printers are the solution. He believes that in fifty years, 3-D printers will decentralize the technology industry. Anyone can make anything for dirt cheap. People will fabricate plastic, iron, aluminum, and more from their closets. "That's real democracy," he concludes. "That's real freedom."

"Man," I say. "Most people, I say something, I have to explain so much. You get it."

He shakes his head. "You have no idea. Sometimes I think I'm crazy."

"Me, too."

"People are stuck in their worlds." He tells me about a guy ISIS burned to death. "It's fucking crazy, man. These fucking idiots. They know nothing about Islam. We're fighting each other for no reason. People are just…"

"It's a political thing," I say. "It's about homogenizing power. We need a society that can accommodate multiple ways of being."

He nods. "Yes. That's it. People need to let people be. Let them live how they want to live."

I sip my mango juice and stare over Kareem's shoulder at an empty table by the door. I suspect Kareem and I are stuck in our worlds, as Uncle Tomás is in his. Two years ago, when the furniture was how it used to be and the kitchen was visible, greasy, and smoking, I sat at that table. This was my first date since Glory. I'm not sure if it was even that. We had met at an MSA gathering, and she'd asked my name.

"Joe," I answered.

"Really?" she replied. Her name was Hakima, and she was tall and thin. She wore a crimson headscarf, and her skin was smooth, ivory white. Her eyes were deep brown and decorated lightly with shadow. Her lips were a subtle shade of pink. She held a half-eaten pizza over her plate and squinted at me. "Where're you from?"

"Connecticut."

"Where're you really from?"

I paused. "Dad's from Pakistan. Mom's from the DR."

"Ah," she said. "There we go. So what's your real name?"

I looked away. "Jihad."

"You should go by that."

I scrunched my nose. "I have to do a lot of explaining. It's easier to just go with Joe. People don't ask questions."

"I think you should go with Jihad. It's a beautiful name. I like what it means. Do you know what it means?"

"It means struggle?" I replied, as if I might be wrong.

We texted a few times afterward. Apparently we both liked the Puerto Rican band Calle 13. My favorite song was "P'al Norte." It is fast and energetic, a loudspeaker for the trials of migration. It made me feel alive. Hers was "La Vuelta al Mundo." It's somber and deliberate, a meditation on the banality of modern life. There is a line about believing, not in the Church, but in a lover's gaze. I think it would work better if Rumi wrote it, if God were her gaze. A few weeks later Hakima asked if I wanted to share a meal sometime. I said yes.

We ate here at the halal dive. Over shawarma, Hakima told me she didn't consider herself Iranian. She didn't believe in national identities.

"My aunt and uncle, they tell me it's in my blood. They tell me, 'You are Iranian. You are one of us.' I don't like that. I'm not in my blood." She gestured with her fork in my direction. "I know more Urdu than my Pakistani friends and more Spanish than my Latino friends." Our eyes met. "Are you fluent?"

I focused on the mint leaves drifting in my Moroccan iced tea. "Not really. I know more Spanish than Urdu. I used to be fluent. When I was like four. Fluent for a four-year-old." I shrugged. "I don't know what happened."

"Don't worry." She smiled. "I'll teach you."

"That would be nice."

"But yeah," she pressed, reading my ambivalence. "I'm not really Iranian, you know?"

"Sure you are," I rebutted. Only an Iranian would describe herself this way. They are as strange as Pakistanis and Dominicans. They too are haunted by their Santiagos, worshipping the devils who made them, the monsters from whose loins they had entered this world. I didn't tell Hakima this. I simply added, "You should be proud of where you came from."

"I'm not so sure." She groaned briefly and exhaled.

"Hey, Persians were the original Aryan race," I teased. "That's something, right?"

Hakima laughed and chewed on a cube of lamb. After a moment she looked up again. "We do so much to each other." She swallowed. "Have you heard of the Yazidis?"

"No."

"They're mostly Kurds, related to pre-Islamic Persian traditions like Zoroastrianism and some esoteric Muslim Sufi orders. People think they're Devil-worshippers, but they're not. Not really. People don't get it. ISIS is doing all kinds of crap to them." She explained that the Yazidis consider the Devil a fallen angel. According to the Qur'an, when God asked Creation to bow to Adam and Eve, the Devil refused. "I am made from higher elements," he declared, "from smokeless fire. Man is made from clay, the dirt of the earth. I am the higher being." Muslims don't believe angels have the free will to disobey God, so the Devil had to be a jinn. But the Yazidis must believe angels are also capable of choice, because their version of the Devil is called the Peacock Angel. In some interpretations of Yazidi mythology, he disobeyed God not only out of arrogance, but also because he refused to bow to anyone except the Lord. Eventually he extinguished the flames of his punishment with his own tears. God forgave him, and he was raised from his fallen state. "It's interesting, isn't it?" Hakima asked me.

I sipped my tea and thought for a while.

"I guess so," I said. "I mean, I think either way the problem is the Devil is a literalist. He thinks the material we're made from determines our moral status. He thinks bowing is worship. He's like these fundamentalists, kind of. He's a literalist. He takes things as they are."

Hakima grinned. It looked as if she was about to wink. "You believe there's a higher reality."

"Yeah."

"I dunno." She adjusted her headscarf. "I like to think we can understand everything rationally. We can figure out God. We can prove things. I consider myself a Mu'tazili."

"Cool," I lied. I had no idea what she meant. Later, I learned about the Mu'tazilis in class. They were an early Islamic school of thought dedicated to rational inquiry. They held the Qur'an as created, noneternal, and finite. At best, the Mu'tazili arguments made for interesting conversation. But I could find no solace in the cold clarity of reason. I didn't know who the Mu'tazilis were then, but I did believe this: No rational argument could prove God. If God could be understood, it was by experience, not proof. God eschewed definition. But I wasn't sure if I had experienced God. I couldn't imagine a thing beyond reason.

There was another long pause. The smell of shawarma and hookah diffused from the open kitchen. Traffic bustled outside. Hakima fiddled with an irregularity in the wood table. She plucked her nail on the grain, chipping red polish onto the tip of her finger.

"Anyway," she began and stopped.

I looked up. So did she. She flattened her lips. "I think we both know why we're here."

I gripped the table and laughed a little bit. I spoke, but the words felt like another's. "I have no idea what you're talking about."

After, I tried to convince myself I was clueless, as I often am. But I think I knew exactly what I was doing. I wanted someone who knows herself. I didn't want Glory, grounded in the cynic's answer to the old paradox of a God who allows death and suffering. I didn't want me, confused about what ground I stood on. Hakima was too much the latter.

"Oh," Hakima said and laughed nervously. "Okay."

I blink. The memory recedes, and Kareem snaps back into focus. He is dark beneath the eyes. He always looks weary. He's spent half of lunch talking about the inefficiency of the university administration, and how they've left most of the department work to him and Manny. "Fucking bureaucracy, man," he says. "They have no idea." He has so many stories. Stories about gunfights in Cairo alleys with the Egyptian police. Stories about his friends in Egypt who only protested when the Internet died because they wanted to watch porn and play *Call of Duty*. Stories about giant scorpions in desert villages, about riding motorbikes deep into the endless sands and lying there beneath the biggest night sky he's ever seen, enveloping him as if he were perched in the cupola of the International Space Station.

"I've been through some serious shit," he says, "and I don't know everything, but I think I have wisdom about these things. I've been through some shit, but God has always been there for me. I'm very grateful for that." It occurs to me that he is a younger, more educated, Egyptian incarnation of Uncle Tomás. I pray for him the same way I pray for my uncle. Regularly and with concern.

Kareem tells me how much he appreciates talking. No one listens to him. No one thinks like he does. He reaches over the steaming chicken and takes my hand. "Love you, man."

"Love you back."

On the walk from lunch, he says he's having relationship problems. A year ago, he married a white girl from Brown who had converted to Islam, but his parents still have not approved the match. He met Harriet when he was working at his father's halal slaughterhouse on Eid. She was interested in Islam and had decided to tag along with a mutual friend from Brown who wanted to see the place. His father's business partner caught Kareem looking at Harriet and dared him to ask her out. So it was that Kareem, clad in an apron smeared with blood and flesh, introduced himself.

"That's too bad about you and Harriet," I tell him, and he grunts assent. I always liked that story. Their first encounter is raw and unexpected, and it reminds me of Dad and his halal business.

Dad has told me about the farms he visits. "Most slaughterhouses are loud," he said after he'd arrived from a business trip last year. "It's horrifying. Animals are screaming. They're terrified. You have to wear earplugs. But the humane ones, you walk in"—he swiped a flat palm through the air—"total silence. There is sukoon. That's how you know they're treating the animals right. The decibel level." He works with Christian farmers in the Midwest, and when he first explained his holistic halal model, they cried. They too sanctified the flesh of the slaughtered. "This is what we have been trying to do for years," they said. "This is how our grandfathers did it. But now it is so hard in this business. It is so hard."

✳

My fridge breaks, and Mom drives into Manhattan with a new one. She calls Uncle Tomás to help me move it in. She brings me home-cooked plátanos y arroz con pollo, and we eat as we wait for Uncle Tomás to arrive. "I told him two o'clock," she says. "He's always getting confused! I told him two o'clock. I don't know what his problem is. I keep telling him, when he dies I'm not going to his funeral!" We eat more. She tells me about the woman who lived next door. "You should ask him about that," she says. "She introduced him to all these bad habits. He was only your age, you know. Twenty, twenty-one. She was maybe twenty-six. She was married and everything." Veronica was the friend of a cousin from the Dominican Republic. My abuelos had helped her and her newlywed husband find a place in New York.

Uncle Tomás arrives and argues with Mom about the time. "Your mother, boy," he says, "she's a pain in the ass, you know that?" He pauses. "But she has a good heart." We haul the fridge up the stairs, and afterward he sits and breathes like a dog. "I need a smoke," he says, patting the pack in his breast pocket. "Man I need a smoke." He leaves for ten minutes then returns to help me lift the fridge the rest of the way.

I ask him about the neighbor. He is motionless for a minute, gears stripping their teeth somewhere behind his skull. Finally his eyebrows jump. "Oh! That one. Uh ... uh ... Veronica? Veronica. You wanna know about that chick?"

"Yeah," I say.

"Oh, I'll tell you about her. She was hot, boy. She was so fucking hot."

"Did she have anything to do with the Devil?"

He laughs and coughs from his chest. "Shit, boy. What do you think? Everything has to do with that son of a bitch."

As Uncle Tomás speaks, I remember Mom's account of how the family landed in Washington Heights at the apartment on 169th Street. First it was 135th in Spanish Harlem, then 175th. And finally they were across from New York Presbyterian perched on the highest floor overlooking Fort Washington Ave. Before they arrived there, they had many neighbors on 135th Street, some of whom I know today. Their Puerto Rican neighbor Carmen, who later moved to the third floor on 169th, still specializes in Dominican cakes, heavy with rich icing and filled with homemade guava jelly.

Veronica I don't know. She was a family friend, and as they had with many families, the Paolis helped her relocate to Manhattan. She had recently married when she moved onto their street. Uncle Tomás tells me he noticed her several times. She was only a few years older but, unlike Tomás, she had grown into her body. Her jaw had set, wide and firm, and she had bleached her hair blond many times. She was blonder even than Tomás, who had by this age shifted naturally into a light shade of brown. She always wore dark-red lipstick, high heels, and a golden necklace that dangled a bulky crucifix between her breasts. "She had big breasts," Uncle Tomás confirms. "Like mountains." Her ass, he concedes, was as flat as his.

Veronica lived on the first floor of the apartment building next door. Every day when he walked home from work, Tomás would pass her place. She would set up a lawn chair in her living room and open the window. Veronica would sprawl her legs across the thin, striped linen and into the space between the window frame and its outward-jutting metal cage. She'd stare out, tapping cigarette ash into a stained wineglass. Her toenails glinted in the afternoon light, when the sun reached the right angle in the sky, and Tomás would stare at the faint line of dark skin that circled above her ankle bones like an old burn mark. She reeked of hard alcohol and thick jasmine perfume. Her neck was lined with parallel scars, gray and faded, as if an animal had dragged her with both paws by the throat when she was a child. Uncle Tomás runs his ashen fingers along the sides of my neck. "Like this, boy," he says to me. "Right along there." I flinch and rub my throat.

He continues.

"Tomás," Veronica would say, smiling at him as he passed.

Her eyes were a fierce shade of brown, almost as blond as her bleached hair, so that in the sunset they appeared orange. Her eyeliner was black. "How are you today?"

"I-I–" Tomás would stutter. "I-I am o-okay."

He would hurry to his apartment and watch Dolores play with her coloring books.

The day the neighborhood boys lodged a pickax in his chest, Tomás paused for a long minute by her window. The window was closed and the shades were drawn, but he could smell her even over the aroma of Carmen's cake drifting from her window a half block down. He fingered the bandage beneath his T-shirt and watched the shadows in the crack between the curtains. They flickered along the edge.

Interested, boy?

Tomás shook his head. He tells me he was very interested. He tells me he played it cool. "Hell no," he told the demon's voice. But I don't think it went down that way. Mom has told me what he was like then. That before 1967 he was always a big baby, clueless, blond, tall, and smooth-skinned as a dolphin. She's told me about the kids who bullied him for his stutter. "Nineteen sixty-seven is the year he started to figure things out," she has said to me many times. "He acts like he's stupid, Tomás, and he is. But he's a survivor too. He knows how to get his way. He's always asking for money, and he always waits for when he thinks I'll be more inclined to give him something. He's like that. He's smart like that. When he met that woman he became what he is. A survivor. He learned it from her. She was a lot like him, you know. A lot like how he would become."

I think Uncle Tomás was terrified. I think he trembled on the sidewalk until Carmen finished baking and the shadows disappeared and the stitches in his chest began to itch.

Over the following weeks, Veronica left him hints. She would wink at him when they crossed paths on the street. She once offered him a cigarette. He declined. When she joined the family for dinner, she would lean over the table in his direction so that all he could see was the crucifix swinging across the abyss of her cleavage. "Tomás would blush and look away," Mom tells me later. "Of course we never knew about all this until years after. But it makes sense now when I remember it. Crazy, though." Uncle Tomás doesn't mention this to me.

He says that sometime in September, he reached her window and Veronica waved at him.

"I-I'm o-okay," he said automatically.

She laughed and beat the air with her cigarette. Ash circled motes of red dust.

"No no no no, Tomás. I need a little help," she said in Spanish. "My sink is broken, and my husband is away for the month. Would you mind?"

"Y-you should call a plumber."

She turned her head and raised an eyebrow. "Is that necessary?"

He shrugged. "I-I guess so."

"Tomás," she began. She stuffed her cigarette into her glass and sat upright. "You do understand?" She looked at him. "You get it, Tomás?"

Tomás raised his hands to express his confusion.

She rolled her eyes, stood, and pushed the lawn chair backward into her apartment. It complained softly against the wood floor. Her face filled the window, obscured by smoke.

"Come on," she said. "I'll buzz you in." She strode into the depths of her apartment.

Tomás stood on the sidewalk and scratched his ear. A sliver of orange sunlight lingered on the street. It streaked across the buildings at waist height. The light blurred and the wall shuddered. He heard humming and the clanking of heavy metal.

"Come on," she beckoned again from somewhere in the apartment. The apartment entrance droned. She must have had her finger pressed against the buzzer.

The clanking stopped, and the light faded. Tomás stepped around the corner, swung open the buzzing door, and followed Veronica into her apartment. The entrance was dark for a moment before she flicked a switch. The door shut behind Tomás. He turned, startled by the noise. When he turned back, she had undone her dress, and her bra was slipping from her breasts. Clothes pooled around her bare ankles. All he saw was flesh.

At this point, I stop Uncle Tomás. "Really?" I say.

"Yeah!" He smirks. "What was I supposed to do? I turn around and she took off everything and she just says my name. She just keeps saying my name and talking about my hair. And I'm like, 'What? What the fuck?' But boy. She was butt naked! Nothing. Zip. Nada. What was I supposed to do?"

"Uh."

His eyebrows jump. "What the fuck was I supposed to do?" He leans close and bares his crooked teeth. "You know what we did, boy?"

"I can guess." I try not to look into the dark, stinky cavity between his ash-stained lips.

"We did it. We fucking did it, boy. You know." He gestures with his hands as if he hasn't made it clear enough. "Capisce?"

"Yeah, I get it." I give myself a few inches to breathe.

"Good."

Afterward, his body tingled, and his heart beat so hard he feared a geyser of blood would erupt again through the stitches in his chest. He lay beside Veronica on the couch as she ran a finger in circles along his shoulder. Her skin was hot and sticky against his. The chandelier swayed in the hot breeze from the open window. Someone called across the street.

Veronica sat up with her back against the arm of the couch. The leather squeaked as she shifted. Tomás lifted his head and rested it on the inside of her thigh. She was now heavy and slick with sweat. He closed his eyes. Beads of perspiration tickled his temples. He felt long, bony fingers slide through the hairs on his chest. They stopped at the stitches.

"Tell me about this," Veronica whispered.

Tomás raised his head. Veronica had picked a box of cigarettes from the coffee table and was knocking one into her palm. Her bleached hair reached from her skull at every angle like one of Dolores's drawings of the rays of the sun. Behind her, the demon perched on the armchair and angled his neck against the ceiling. His tubes hung loose, and he had tucked his morion against the crook of his waist, where he'd sheathed his sword. The demon snapped something from his belt and raised his arm toward Veronica. He held a lighter between his index and thumb, puny in his armored fingers, and flicked. Veronica winked at Tomás and stuck the cigarette between her lips. She leaned sideways into the flame. The demon waited a moment, nodded, closed the lighter, reclined. He picked a crumb from his mustache, dropped it onto his outstretched tongue, and chewed.

"What—?" Tomás screamed. He pushed away, but Veronica pressed her free hand against the side of his head, pinning him to her thigh. He thrashed, breathing sweat and jasmine.

"He's a friend," she assured him.

He quieted and breathed.

"That thing—he—he … He is the Devil."

She shrugged and blew smoke.

"He w-wants to kill me."

The cigarette glowed red as she inhaled and turned toward the demon. "That true, dear?"

The demon smiled and stepped from the armchair. Like an overgrown child, he hobbled on his knees across the living room. His tubing dangled to and fro and his sheath scraped across the floor. The chandelier chimed, cutlery rattled, cupboards shook. He stopped behind the couch and wheezed. He whacked his breastplate. "Piece of shit…" he whispered, barely audible, as he turned. The suit grated against itself. He curled his fingers over the edges of the couch and pressed his weight onto it.

"No," he murmured, looking at Tomás. His smile had faded. "Not true anymore. I dunno. I told you, didn't I? I can't kill you, boy. But I can make you miserable. You've made me miserable. You know that? Yes, you have. You've made me very, very miserable. Boy. What do you have to say for yourself?"

Tomás stared at him, then at Veronica.

"Is—is this for real?" he asked her.

She frowned and nodded, brow raised. "'Course it is, honey."

"No," Tomás corrected, louder now. "I'm saying, is this guy for real?" They looked at him, eyes scrunched between wrinkled flesh. He raised his head and moved Veronica's legs so they bent and pushed up against her breasts. "I'm saying, this motherfucker. He thinks he c-can do what he wants. I'm done, man. Me and God—me and God. We got a plan. God got a plan for me. And for you. And you know me. You kn-know me. You know I'm gonna do God's plan." He stood, fists raised. "You wanna fight? Is that what you want?"

The demon let go of the couch and leaned onto his haunches as it teetered. He laughed. Spittle sprinkled his tubing.

"Tomás," he whispered, "we already have." He looked away. "We already have. You won. You wouldn't remember how it was that you killed me. You were hardly a fetus then. Does that make you happy, Tomás? It makes me extremely unhappy. I want you to know how unhappy it makes me. I want you to know death."

The demon shook his head and continued to stare through the cupboards. He moaned to himself as if regretting a shameful deed. "This kid," he kept saying. "This kid. No matter what I try…" He strode toward the chandelier, where light prismed through beads of glass, and kneeled. He stuck his morion onto his bald scalp and punched his chin. The tubes retracted into the suit. "No matter what I try…" he whispered again, muffled behind the layers of metal. A shard of phosphorescence reached from a bead of glass, moving in tendrils of yellow and orange, and paused before the demon's mask. The demon shrunk around his girth until he was needle thin. The light sucked him into ether.

Veronica curled into a ball and stared at her cigarette. Smoke haloed around her. Her jasmine scent had long since departed. "You smoke?"

Tomás shook his head.

"Open," she said and extended a hand. She placed the cigarette between his lips. "Breathe," she said. He coughed.

She moved the cigarette away and, after a moment, back. "That's right. That's good. Very good, honey. You're getting the hang of this thing." She smiled. "Don't worry about Santiago. I'm here for you. Don't worry about him. Trust me. He's as confused as you are."

A week passed. Tomás would sneak down the street to spend nights with Veronica. They would smoke for hours and watch the moon. She drew bottles of hard liquor from her nightstand and shared. It burned in his throat, but he got used to it. He enjoyed it very much actually. It sent him somewhere else. Somewhere outside of himself. After two weeks, she rolled him his first joint. "You want reality?" she said, handing it over. "That's as real as it gets." He took it, closed his lids, felt his eyeballs roll. He looked inside of himself and glimpsed colors in the dark, spotted and discrete, smaller than particles of sand in the Dominican surf. They were the building blocks that made him and Veronica, her body and his, and everything else he knew. The DR. Manhattan. The sea and the buildings and the sky and the dirt beneath them. "R-real," he agreed.

As Uncle Tomás recounts his story, I remember what Titi Lourdes told me last Easter. She told me about the years before he got arrested, after his last girlfriend overdosed, when he still roomed with Titi Lourdes in the Washington Heights apartment on 169th. Danny and Monica used to live there with Marcos and his sisters, but they moved out because of Uncle Tomás. Titi Lourdes said she would get up in the middle of the night and stumble into the kitchen for a glass of water, and she'd see a woman—a different woman each time—meandering through the hallway between the clothesline. "He was bringing prostitutes into the house!"

she exclaimed to me. "My God." It always smelled strange in his room. Something that wasn't cigarette smoke. "You know what that means," Titi Lourdes told me. "He got off alcohol, but the doctor never said anything about drugs! He does these things, Tomás." Sometimes she would glimpse the feet of the women as they passed the open kitchen door. "Maybe I was half asleep," Titi Lourdes confessed, gripping my arm, "but I swear. I swear sometimes—sometimes the ankles were, you know—" She thrust her wrist into the air and twisted it as far around as she could. "Sometimes the ankles were the other way. Like they were walking backward. But they were not." She shook her head and tightened her grip. "Coño. The scariest thing. I don't know. Maybe I was dreaming. But I know what I saw. I know what I saw. He brought all kinds of monsters into our home."

When he was released from prison, she refused to let him return. He lived in a homeless shelter for a year and then got a room in an apartment somewhere in the Bronx with a landlady who's always high on weed.

After we finish with the fridge, Uncle Tomás and I wait outside for Mom to find a new parking spot. He tells me that when he was sleeping with Veronica back in 1967, he would wake up sometimes and he'd find the demon sitting on a stool at the foot of the bed. He'd have his visor down and a fist locked beneath his chin.

"G-get out," Tomás would hiss.

The demon would laugh. "Where is there to go?"

One night the demon did not laugh. Instead, he unhinged his mask, drew his sword, and twirled it through the ambient light that seeped through the curtains. The sword was thin and long and patterned with cursive Latin except for three words in block letters.

LIBERTE   EQUALITE   FRATERNITE

He whispered something about the throat of a circumcised dog and slid the sword down through the mattress between Tomás and Veronica. Veronica stirred. The demon waited for her breathing to steady, then faced Tomás.

"Tomorrow," he said, "her husband will return from California." He bent the hilt of his sword in her direction. "She will end this in the morning, at dawn, before coffee—"

"Sh-shut your mouth," Tomás interrupted.

The demon wagged a finger. It tinkled as if jangling a ring of heavy keys.

"No can do, Tomás. Man up. This was never anything. This was nothing to her. This was a fling."

"No." His voice rose. "Not t-true."

The demon chuckled and stared down the blade.

"You have no idea..." He left the sword in the mattress and slunk to Veronica's side of the bed. He leaned on the edge of the mattress and peered over her breasts. "My boy," he said. "My boy. You are so easily moved. You think you have bested me? You believe this is over? This is far from over, Tomás." He gestured at Veronica's body, arms sprawled, hair askew. "I am above all this ... this pettiness. I am not flesh, Tomás. I am fire. Watch. You watch and you will see. Your flesh will be your undoing. It already has. Achilles' weakness was never his heel. It was that he had a heel at all. It was that he had a body. His weakness was carnal, boy, don't you see?" He reached over Veronica's body, drew the sword, and tucked it beneath Tomás's chin. "It's done, my boy. I will die. I died. I die. So be it. You will live, have lived, live at the cost of this." He pricked Tomás's skin. "This will rot, but I will always burn."

He strode out of the room. Tomás clutched his bleeding neck and fought the urge to weep. Be a man, he told himself. Be a man.

Uncle Tomás lights a cigarette. "Still haven't figured out, though—who the hell is Achilles?"

"The Trojan War," I explain.

"Oh! Yeah. Brad Pitt from, uh, that movie."

"Yeah," I say.

"But anyway, that wasn't everything," Uncle Tomás tells me.

In the morning Veronica ended it, and he clenched his jaw and blinked a few times even though his eyes were already red. He waited a minute.

"Tell me how to find him," he demanded.

"Who?"

"You know who."

"You think I know where to find him?" She scoffed and quieted. "You really think I know where to find him. You really do, don't you? You *are* a retard."

Tomás leaned from the end of his chair, fingers trembling along the edge of the table. "Tell me. Or-or-or I'm not going." He glanced at the door. He would wait for her husband to return.

"Are you blackmailing me, honey? Your mother—"

He shook his head. "I c-can take a beating. Can you? Eh?"

She sipped her coffee. In the morning light she was dark and her features bony. Her mascara had bled onto her cheeks, and her hair hung loose around her shoulders. It looked to Tomás as if she'd spent a day climbing coconut palms. She scrunched her nose and lips into contusions of shriveled skin.

"Eh?" he repeated.

"I can take a beating, Tomás." Finally she faced him. "But I suppose, for the sake of..." She smiled briefly. Away from sunlight, her eyes were dark and crystalline. "I suppose everyone's got a beef with the Devil." She touched his arm. "There is a place he goes when he wants to get away from ... this." She encompassed the room with a sweep of her arm. "From this world. Like a monk in his temple. He does behave like a loner, right? I guess it makes sense. Santiago is a thinker. He does not like this world. It's distracting, tedious, burdensome. He wants to make us see that. That's where you'll find him, in the place outside of space and time. Follow my instructions carefully, Tomás. Are you listening? This is no joke, Tomás."

"Uh-huh." He grinned stupidly.

Veronica pinched him, and he sat straight. "Riverside Park at midnight. Look for the beach chair in the woods. Do not talk to the man on the rock. He is not a drug dealer. I tried once." She gestured across the length of her body. "That's how I got like this. Talked to the wrong guy. I used to be happy in Santo Domingo. I didn't do crazy shit, and I didn't sleep around—"

"You sleep around?" Tomás demanded, ears perked.

She glared. "You think you're the first? Or the last? You think you're so fucking special?" She rubbed her thumb and raised a shaking finger to her brow. "I miss our country. I miss the water. I was better then. At least that is how I remember it. I get confused sometimes..."

Mom arrives before Uncle Tomás can continue.

"Stop it, Tomás! Don't fill him with these things," she says. To me: "Don't listen to him. You know your Uncle Tomás. You know how he gets."

✳

Glory haunts me the way Veronica haunts Uncle Tomás.

Both inserted themselves into our lives, eager to pursue relationships they would end shortly thereafter. Like Uncle Tomás, I felt taken along for a ride I could not control or predict, compelled by Glory's forward character, by the idea of our flesh, and by the prospect of not being alone. I don't know if this was love.

I first asked Glory out on her eighteenth birthday. I was still seventeen. I bought her a copy of my favorite book, a collection of short stories by Ted Chiang. We had gone paintballing with her friends. I had taken a shot in the pinky finger and was bleeding. I said I was fine, but she insisted we go to her car and clean the wound. She cracked open her bottle and poured water over my finger, applied a napkin, and wrapped a Band-Aid around the bruised skin. She pressed her lips to the soft plastic and looked at me. I should have kissed her then. We returned to the rest area, where she sat above me on the bench and toyed with my necklace. She brought it around and inspected the tiny calligraphy etched across the aqeeq.

"What's this?" she whispered in my ear.

"I dunno," I said, pretending not to take it seriously. "It's called the Four Quls. It's supposed to keep away the Evil Eye or something like that. It's from the, uh, ... the Qur'an."

"Oh," she said.

Afterward everyone drove back to her place. Our socks and sweaters were logged with water and paint, so we slipped them off and sat barefoot on her lawn. I crossed my legs, and Glory leaned into my lap. We had started holding hands a week ago when she invited me to movie night with her friends. She had been inviting me all year. The night I went, they were watching *Let the Right One In,* the original Swedish version, about a socially castigated ten-year-old who falls in love with a vampire girl who looks the same age. I don't like vampire movies and cheap horror flicks, but this was good. It wasn't scary. It was brooding and atmospheric. By some point during the film, Glory's hand was in mine, and she was reaching across her body to rub my arm. I was losing focus when suddenly the girl stood naked on screen, revealing dark hair between her legs. "That's great," I said, averting my gaze. "That's really great." Glory laughed. I've since looked it up. Apparently there was nothing there. A scar marked the place where her genitalia should have been.

On the lawn, I burrowed my nose in Glory's hair. She smelled of paint. I explained my scattered lines theory. "If we live in a universe of three dimensions in space and one in time, perhaps there's like a parallel world of three dimensions of time and one of space. And if they intersect … where do you think they intersect?"

"Tell me," she encouraged.

I moved my hands through the air. "Along straight edges. Lines. Right? The lowest common denominator between the two worlds is one dimension of time and one of space, bound together. That's how you communicate from one to the other. Through a straight line, infinitesimally thin, moving through linear time."

"Cool."

We sat for a while. I remembered her friends had warned me it was about time I asked her out. "Do you want to, uh, go out sometime?"

She turned around and pecked me on the cheek. "Yes, I would."

We decided on a day, a time, and the sushi place on Main

Street. We made out afterward in the parking lot. A group
of boys heckled us from across the road. On our way home
I avoided her eyes and checked my watch.

"It's late," I confessed.

She smiled. "You're going to get in a whole lot of trouble
with me."

My ears burned.

Her words remind me of Veronica's. *Don't you get it,
Tomás?* I know I can never become him. I know it is not in
my blood. I know that I was not born into the circumstances
he was born into. I know that my family frequently prayed
for me when I was little, that I was one of the youngest
cousins and the straight-A student and the Good Muslim
and a pampered child on both sides of the family. But I
am afraid that I will become like him. That I will grow old
alone and horny.

As Veronica did for Tomás, Glory would bare her body for
me, leading me down a path from which I feared I could not
turn. I committed myself to her. I told her I didn't want to
have sex, which she said she was okay with, but I let the idea
lose definition as weeks passed. I chose to ignore the maxim
among ulema to avoid the doubtful. Sex is penetration, I
convinced myself at last. The rest is fair game. When I told
her this, Glory chuckled and said, "Then I guess I already
lost my virginity to a tampon." The summer after senior year,
we would go out to dinner and movies. Afterward we'd park
somewhere remote and make out for a while. She would
help me strip off her clothes and then lie beneath me in the
backseat of her car.

"What do you want me to do?" I'd say in a small voice.

"Whatever you want," she'd say.

"What do you *want* me to do?" I'd say again, confused.

"Do whatever you want."

She would lie back and close her eyes. I'd start by kissing her, and after a minute or two she would make suggestions. We were polite about it. "Can I touch you here?" we'd ask each other. We would ask who preferred the top or bottom. I preferred the latter. Partly I didn't like moving around. Mostly it was because of my butt. I was self-conscious about it. I didn't want her to see my fat hairy ass dangling in the air. My ass might be the most Dominican thing about me.

She'd ask me questions about God. One night I told her what our imam Dr. Tariq says, that God is Al-Wadud, The Most Affectionate. Al-Wadud is often translated as The Most Loving, but Dr. Tariq claims this is inadequate. "It is so much more," he likes to say. "Love has an opposite. Hate. But look in your thesaurus. Affection has no antonym."

Glory made a sound. "I don't know about that," she said.

I remembered that afternoon on her lawn after paintball. She had slid her fingers over the bridge of my foot and through my toes. "That tickles," I said. She asked if I'd broken my foot when I was little. I hadn't. I still haven't broken a bone in my body. Neither has Dad, though we both have a habit of breaking things. We underestimate our strength.

"I was born like that," I said. "Why?"

She pressed her foot against mine. The shape of hers was smooth. Mine was bony, wide, and thickly veined like a Cro-Magnon's.

"See? Most people's feet aren't like that," she explained. "I've never seen a foot like yours."

"I had no idea."

She traced the bone of my big toe. We stared at it, and

our breathing slowly synchronized. With each minute the bone seemed more alien, older, as if it had sprung from a prehistoric seed in my blood, carried dormant from generation to generation across land and sea, body to body, until at last it manifested as calcium and flesh.

the last memory

Glory and I spoke over the phone a year or two into undergrad. I was having girl trouble.

"How do I, uh, how do I, uh..." I searched for the word. "You know. How do I woo women?"

"How did you woo me?"

"I wooed you?"

Her sigh emerged as static. "Joe, what do girls like?"

"I don't know."

An outburst of bitter laughter. "Girls like chocolate and pussy," she explained.

"Ah," I said. "Okay." I wasn't sure how that was supposed to help.

I dredged through memories of Glory and was surprised to realize the prevalence of both. I guess I shouldn't have been. Mom would buy chocolate truffles from Balducci's for me to give to Glory, and she loved them. We'd feed each other on late nights in her Jeep.

We broke up a week after my parents and I returned from an Islamic retreat in Turkey. I brought her a box of chocolates from a Turkish delight store outside the docks of the Bosphorus. An inscription by Rumi decorated the box, but she didn't linger on it. We went out a few nights later, and afterward we drove to a parking lot by the beach. The Long Island Sound was dark, quiet, glistening. I fingered her and nuzzled my nose in the hair between her legs. I knew this smell like my own. I would always know it, like the wind and salt off the water on a summer day or the sand in our hair. Heat rose from her, thick as the haze above the asphalt of a forlorn highway in the DR.

As she climaxed, I extended the tip of my tongue slowly until I felt her. A moment passed, she clenched, and then she released, body limp against the backseat.

She raised me by the sides of my head and pressed her lips to mine.

"That was amazing," she said. "Thank you."

"It was only for a second." I blushed. She had always wanted this, but I had refused on principle.

"No." She kissed me again. "It was amazing." She held me apart. "What made you change your mind?"

I avoided her gaze and concentrated on the cars passing the intersection beyond the woods. "I missed you," I said in a small voice. "I missed you a lot." I pressed my chest against her bare breasts. She thanked me again, but this time her diction was succinct. "For what?" I asked.

She gestured at the intersection. A car's headlights had passed through the Jeep.

"For covering me."

"Oh," I said. She knew I hadn't noticed the car, as we both knew that I had embraced her for another reason. We left the realizations unspoken. I tucked her hair behind her ear. "Would you mind doing me?"

"Are you okay with that now?"

"Yeah."

She kneeled. I told her to stop when I couldn't hold back any longer.

"Oh my god," I said.

"Now you know why guys like this so much," she said, smirking.

A few days later she ended it on a rainy day over Subway sandwiches. She explained that we were different people who liked different things. I told her I felt the same, which was true, but had lacked the courage to act on my doubt. She was a white girl skeptical of God who rowed crew and drove her own car. I was a mixed-race bookworm selectively confident about my faith and an only child. She talked about pheromones and castrated flower genitals and red tape. I talked about socialism and love and the possibility of extraterrestrial life. But I supposed it was about more than that. Or perhaps less.

Over the phone, Glory had described it in three words. *Chocolate and pussy.*

I close my eyes and remember the night in the parking lot. The memory is vivid but dreamlike. Once or twice, in that memory, I've glimpsed a woman submerged in the Sound and, in the sparse woods between the Jeep and the intersection, the reflection of moonlight on something large and black, as if a mangled incarnation of Arthur C. Clarke's monolith is lodged in the mulch. I consider these recollections fabricated, but I wonder if my case is the opposite. Perhaps until now I have refused to recognize what I saw or what I was not prepared to see. I wonder if, in telling his story, Uncle Tomás is hearing it for the first time. Is he now realizing what he refused to remember? I am too afraid to ask.

I recall a previous night when Glory and I discovered a raccoon ogling us from the perch of a nearby fence. It observed with quiet, dronelike attention, eyes glowing in the dark. Its poise was as otherworldly as my last memories of Glory.

I know now that Santiago is not new to me. I know that he has always waited in the shadows of my memories and my predecessors'. He is catching up to me, traveling forward faster than I age. He careens through linear space and linear time, waiting to free himself from history with his bulky suit and his morion and his Spanish sword. LIBERTE EQUALITE FRATERNITE.

✳

Recently, I've decided to grow a beard. I figure it has something to do with the body being integral to the self. I believe it will make me more of a man.

4. FIRE

✳

It is snowing during spring break when Uncle Tomás calls. He speaks with Mom for less than a minute. She hangs up. "That was Tomás," she announces. Usually when they talk he wants money, and usually they argue loudly. Mom is smiling. Dad and I look up from the dining room table. We're eating breakfast.

"What was he saying?" I ask.

"Oh, nothing." She laughs. "I have no idea why, but he always calls me when it snows."

✳

I am waiting to meet a professor when a message from Glory pops into my inbox. There is no subject. I open the email and read. "Hey Joe," she begins. She has only written a few lines. Her father passed away, and she tried to make it to Connecticut from school in Pennsylvania, but he died before the bus got anywhere close. She had seen him a few days beforehand, when she'd read him her favorite short story, "The Merchant and the Alchemist's Gate" by Ted Chiang. I had introduced her to the author years ago, but she only read his work after we'd broken up. The story is set in medieval Baghdad. It is about a man who returns to his past in an attempt to undo his misdeeds. He realizes he cannot change his past, but the experience of having relived it strengthens his moral resolve. Chiang ends with a beautiful passage about self-forgiveness and God's mercy. The concept was inspired by Kip Thorne's ideas about the causal geometry of wormholes. Glory tells me she feels like the time traveler in the story, that perhaps her fate was to miss her father's passing. Perhaps it was meant to be. She hopes her father understood the story when she read it to him the last time they spoke. She says the funeral is this weekend, and I should come if I'm around town. She misses talking.

I sit down outside my professor's office and stare at my phone. I've been thinking about her recently because of Uncle Tomás and Santiago's visitations in both of our lives. It is strange that this happened now.

I talk with my professor, but my mind is elsewhere. I'm thinking about wormholes and astrolabes. I want to grieve, but I didn't know her father well. I try to imagine what it would be like to lose mine. Speculation pushes through the folds of my memory.

I erase the thought. The idea alone is too devastating. I cannot imagine losing Dad.

I rub my nose and hold my papers against my knee.

In my room I toss my backpack on the floor and perform my ablutions. I stand for a second, mind blank and water tickling my skin, before I slip my kufi around my hair, face northeast, and raise my thumbs behind my ears. I recite the words of God. Typically I pray in silence, but today I close my eyes and murmur the words aloud.

in the name of god the most gracious the most merciful
praise be to god lord of the worlds

The Arabic tumbles from my throat. My pronunciation is uneven, but I allow my recollection of the words to carry me forward. My body follows. It guides me through the movements, and I obey the memory in my flesh. I am somewhere else in the darkness behind my eyes. Often I rush, my mind elsewhere. But today I savor every motion and every word. I can feel nothing except these words at this continuous moment. Thought dissipates. I have the fleeting sensation that I am not a passerby in this body, that I do not occupy it, but that it constitutes me. As the prayer ends, I begin to laugh. I cry quietly. I have rarely felt this close to God.

I draw a string of prayer beads from my pocket and recite the Names of God. I pray for Glory and her family and her father. I clutch the wooden beads in hand and curl so my forehead hovers above the prayer mat and my chin brushes my knees.

to god do we belong and to god shall we return

I wonder if I miss Glory, but I don't. Not now. I care that we meant something to each other beyond our flesh. I realize now that we did.

After several minutes I run out of all the Names I know. I sway on my knees. I don't want this moment to end. I have felt a place beyond pain, beyond grief, beyond history. Al-Ghazali describes prayer and recitation as technologies of the self. They are tools for disciplining the flesh. They make the body sacred, shape it for good works and encounters with the divine. Sufis write that the believer is like the moth that encircles the flame, striving to consume itself in the fire. I feel for a brief moment that I have glimpsed this fire from far away.

I run my hands over my face and rise. Outside the window, campus looms above Manhattan. The Hudson shimmers in the moonlight. It is dark everywhere, but there are too many lights. I think of Kareem's motorbike kicking sand in the Egyptian desert beneath the Milky Way. I imagine Uncle Tomás swimming under the belly of the Dominican night.

I look into the opaque sky.

"Thank you," I whisper.

I return to the prayer mat and kneel. I place my forehead on the blue carpet, as I do in every prayer, and breathe fresh dust and lint. This is the best position from which to pray, facing down along the trajectory of gravity, eyes opened, vision darkened by my own shadow. The Prophet said that in this posture, the Devil's whisper is powerless and the believer is closest to God.

"Thank you," I say again. "Thank you thank you thank you."

I don't reply to Glory for two days. I still don't know what to say.

✳

I meet Uncle Tomás at night outside the campus gates. I'm coming off a bad cold, and Mom wants to make sure I carry an inhaler in case I have another asthma attack. I've only ever had two, and it's been at least ten or fifteen years since the last one. Uncle Tomás uses prescription inhalers, and he has a spare.

He hands me a small black bag. He is thick with the stench of ash. I thank him and reach inside. I want to make sure he hasn't used the inhaler. I don't want to press my lips against a surface that his have touched. Sealed gray plastic wraps around the hard L-shaped outline of an inhaler.

"Thanks," I say. I reach up and hug him. "Love you, Uncle Tomás."

"Love you too," he says. He makes as if to turn, then faces me. "By the way, do you have, uh, twenty dollars?"

"You need twenty bucks?"

"Yeah. Your mother, man. She won't give me shit. Don't tell her."

I stare down the infinite metal alley of Amsterdam. Downtown is black and bright. I can give the homeless man on the street the benefit of the doubt, but I know Uncle Tomás. I know how he is with money. He might use the cash for drugs or prostitutes or bootlegged DVDs or cigarettes or Powerball. He sways in front of me, billowing in Amsterdam's wind tunnel, cool air picked from the surface of the Hudson and carried by the movement of traffic and bodies. I shake my head, reach into my wallet, and hand him a twenty-dollar bill.

"There you go," I say.

"Thank you, Jihad."

Before he leaves, I ask him to tell me about the night he snuck into Riverside Park in search of Santiago. I want to know how he faced the Devil. Did he take him out?

He sits on a bench and draws the last cigarette from his breast pocket.

"I've seen some freaky shit," he says. "But this was something else, boy." He is so quiet I can hear his cigarette crackle above the city's roar. "I dunno what I saw, boy. I dunno what the hell I saw..."

✳

Uncle Tomás tells me that after Veronica dumped him, he

slipped from the family apartment at midnight and walked downtown. He entered Riverside Park near 110th and descended onto the path. The park was cold and dark, but columns of lamps extended in either direction along the walkway, an infinite tunnel of pale yellow fire as if he were staring down the throat of a dragon. The light seemed to seep, viscous, into the darkness. It lingered like mist in the night air.

As he approached the tennis courts, he glimpsed a tall, thin figure standing atop a slab of slanted rock at the edge of the woods between the walkway and the street above. He wore a skullcap and clutched a clear plastic bag stuffed with weed. His watch sparkled in the darkness.

"Guy was a fucking weed dealer," Uncle Tomás tells me. "He just stared at me. Kept staring at me like what the hell so I spat at him and kept walking. I went back there, uh, a few years ago. I went walking around during the day and I had to piss and I saw that rock and what was I gonna do? I figured, you know, may as well. Right, boy? So I went to that rock and I went—*sssssss!*" He twists his waist right and then left. "Before I knew it a cop put me in, uh, handcuffs and everything. That was recently. Not then."

That night, Tomás continued past the courts and through the woods. Beyond the lamplights, the park was pitch black. He drew his father's flashlight from his pocket. The trail was narrow and overgrown. Birds moaned from the treetops as he stumbled ahead. He stepped over and below fallen trunks strewn in his way.

He entered a clearing. A large tree spread the dome of its branches overhead. In the middle, a bouquet of litter decorated a broken lawn chair slouched in the dirt. Tomás kicked aside the shards of a shattered bottle, sat in the mulch, and waited for dawn.

He thought about the Devil. The bastard had made his father whip him with his belt and got some kid to stab him with a fucking pickax, and now he'd told his girl they were done. He was going to kill the son of a bitch.

She wasn't your girl. She was never your girl.

Tomás heard the muffled sound of crunching branches and grass ground underfoot. The dirt shook. "I smelled gasoline and, uh, Windex, and I was like, he's here," Uncle Tomás tells me. An incongruent tower of metal rose above him. At night, the demon was almost invisible in his black armor. He shimmered in the moonlight. The metal shifted, and Tomás heard a thump. The visor screeched aside. The demon's pasty, brown-and-red-haired face glowed in the darkness. Pillars of wrinkled skin rose above the crest of his brow. He reached down and flicked Tomás with his thumb. The blow sent Tomás into a dark place alive with red and yellow. He spun through ether, rotating along the axis of his height, squeezed into himself and needle-thin. It was so bright that he wanted to close his eyes, but he remembered vaguely that he was not awake. He continued to whir. He felt his body unwrap, his limbs move in ways he cannot describe to me, and for a moment he felt whole again and he saw stars and he was cold and he couldn't breathe and his lungs, his mighty swimmer's lungs, wanted to collapse. Something big and fiery burned in the near distance, but it was still so, so cold, and he heard a voice—"Shit. Shit shit shit. Medieval fucking suit. Shit shit shit shit."—and something clanked and banged, and again he was spinning through the light of his own ether. At last darkness arrived.

He woke in a dense forest. Thick, gnarled trunks spread as far as he could see. They were stout and white, and the ground beneath them was lush and green but marked by the outlines of roots. He could hear birds chirping in the shallow canopy. The air was sweet, warm, and grassy, but he detected the faint odor of burning wood. He heard a distant roar, regular and smooth, unlike the inconsistent clockwork of New York City. Tomás wondered if a waterfall flowed nearby. Overhead, the sky was pitch black. Something glowed in the distance, radiant as a sun, but he could not see it beyond the canopy's shade.

He wandered for hours. "I kept going and going," Uncle Tomás says to me. "Biggest forest I ever seen." Soon he glimpsed pastures on the horizon, flat and swaying with long grass. "I've never seen grass that shiny. Going back and forth in the wind like, uh, seaweed underwater." Cattle moved like clouds over the distant plain.

Tomás exited the woods, waded through the pasture, and climbed a hill. He turned around. The stout forest spread across the land, pockmarked with clearings and bordered by narrow pastures and hills. In the distance, flame rose from the trees. The bonfire was tall and broad as a small city, and it spewed black smoke into the black sky. There were no stars in this sky. It was featureless and dark. The flame alone provided light in this place. Tomás shivered in the wind and breathed. The air was crisp, and for a moment he forgot the smell of ash.

A figure approached the base of the hill. Tomás nestled into the grass and sat watching. It began as a gray-clothed sliver that zigzagged upward. Every few moments it would pause and then begin again. Minutes passed, and it took shape. At first Tomás mistook it for Miguelito. The shoulders were stocky and wide as his brother's. But the face materialized, and Tomás, shaking his head, could not unsee the image of Carlos's face, serene and Italian, round-jawed and clean-shaven except for the layer of hair above his lip. He was tall, taller maybe than Tomás, and he was wearing gray overalls smeared with dirt and oil.

Tomás stood, arms folded across his chest, but as soon as the man reached the plateau atop the hill, his likeness changed again. The man looked like Tomás, lanky and dirty-blond, except that he wore brown-rimmed spectacles. Tomás opened and closed his mouth. "I-I—"

The man stopped in front of Tomás, smiled, and stood beside him. He smelled of coal.

"Wh-who are you?" Tomás asked.

The man spoke in Spanish. He pronounced his words gently and with care. "I am a miner for Alcoa," he explained, staring across the canopy of the forest. "I mine bauxite in Barahona. Bauxite is our future. It is a kind of aluminum. In fact it is the world's greatest source of aluminum. Aluminum is in everything. It is the stuff of soda cans and cars, tanks and rockets. The first man on the moon will get there because of the red ore I tore from the guts of my country. He might not know, but I will."

He looked away.

As Uncle Tomás tells his story, I recall what Titi Lourdes told me at Christmas. She said that Abuelo had been the first Alcoa employee in the Dominican Republic. "It was a jungle then," she explained. "They gave him so much money." He would help Alcoa hire the unemployed and offer destitute men living wages. They razed the jungle valleys and dug where they found bauxite deposits in the red soil.

On Amsterdam, Uncle Tomás coughs from deep in his

chest. He wrestles the tar in his lungs for several minutes. Then he sucks on his cigarette, moans contentedly, and continues.

The miner explained to him that loose rock had caved him inside a mine a few days ago. He discovered an alternate route to the surface.

"The path led me through the Sierra de Bahoruco, beneath the water I think," the miner concluded, "and here I am. When I emerged, I soon realized that I was no longer in Barahona. I fed on the cooked carcasses of pigeons left in the wake of the primordial flame. I pity the creatures. Tell me, do you work for Alcoa? You are not wearing a miner's uniform. Are you management? You are too young for management."

The miner looked at Tomás expectantly.

Tomás raised his palms beside either ear as if to deflate a threat.

"I-I am from the capital city," he explained. "My father worked for Alcoa. I live in New York now. I work at, uh, Fairway Market."

"Ah," the miner replied. "Then your father must have taught you something about geology and nature." He leaned into Tomás's shoulder and pointed at the forest. "You see this forest? It is called a trembling aspen. The forest is one tree only. The roots from the original travel through the ground and sprout everywhere. They are each genetically identical. I wonder which is the first. The aspen is clearly a very old creature to be so large."

"Uh-huh," Tomás said.

The miner wrapped an arm around him and squeezed. "Relax, my friend. It is a beautiful thing. Do you see the flame?" He gestured into the fire. It rose, mountainous, from the aspen and billowed miles above the canopy. "It gives this land life. By its light, the aspen grows. But see also that the flame burns only by the wood of the same organism. The aspen consumes itself just as it is its own sustainer."

Tomás shrugged the miner's arm from his shoulder.

"Listen, man, I didn't come h-here for this shit. I c-came for the Devil. Do you know him?"

The miner smiled and turned so that he faced Tomás. "Santiago? I believe he gets a bad rap. He has misled himself as much as he has misled others."

Tomás ground his teeth. "He-he hates me. He's the Devil, man. He's the Dev—"

The miner raised a finger. "I must stop you here," he interrupted, raising his voice. Tomás quieted. "He is dead, my friend. You do know that? He was the caretaker of this land." The miner explained that on his third day in this place he had stood atop this hill. Down in the pasture—"There," he murmured with tender assurance—a man in a big black marine diver's suit had stumbled from the woods carrying the sweat-drenched body of the miner's wife. He had met Santiago several times before then over his last few days in this place. The demon had spoken often about a curse on the miner's family, that a man who tore the earth from his land might as well tear the flesh from his skin. The demon had feigned hospitality, but the miner had remained suspicious. Why, after all, did he not lead him back to Barahona? He realized, that day, that Santiago was a vengeful demon. He wished to cut short the miner's seed, to make him watch his own flesh, his own child, ripped from its mother's womb.

The miner's wife was dressed in her loose white gown. She was not due for six months, but she moaned as if in labor. Even from here her screaming swam to him against the tide of the wind. The miner rushed from the hill, tears streaming down his face. He had wandered this land for only a few days, but he had worked in Barahona for two weeks before that, so he missed her greatly. The man in the metal diver's suit laid the miner's wife in the grass and shed his bulky garment. Metal collapsed into the earth and sent a stray pigeon skyward. Santiago stepped from the black iron carcass, taller than the aspen, and rested on all fours at the wife's toes. Above him the flame twisted in the near distance, orange and cartoonish against the black. Its heat overcame the miner as if he held his face above hot ore. Santiago spread his wife's legs, lifted her nightgown, and crawled forward. With pursed lips and wet trembling eyes, he reached into the shadow between her thighs.

The miner was nearly upon them. The air buzzed, and the ground shook the miner face-first into dirt. When he rose Santiago lay sprawled in the grass. He flailed and wheezed and his eyes rolled and the miner tried to hold him down, but something cracked. Santiago's flesh began to smolder. The miner turned to his wife. Her eyes were closed and her breathing regular. Beads of sweat trickled along her skin. He placed four fingers beneath her belly button and rested his ear there against her nightgown. Energy thrummed through her skin and the cloth and reverberated in his ear. He could not explain how he knew, he told Tomás, but he did: Their child lived. He then pressed his lips to his wife's and held this pose for a time, feeling the heat radiate from her skin. Reluctantly, he carried her to the diver's suit and placed her inside. He had watched the demon operate the device, and he knew that it transported its contents from one time and place to the next. But he did not know how.

He leaned over Santiago. The demon was fixed in a contorted position, his left arm twisted and legs pointing in the wrong directions. His limbs shook gently like those of an insect caught in a spider's web. His face, too, was frozen in the middle of some great effort, nose scrunched, mustache askew, chin furrowed. Only his eyes and lips moved, twitching but not vacant. Tears slid down toward his ears. He stared into the aspen and with visible struggle clenched his right fist. He groaned. The miner followed his gaze. A figure crouched behind the trunks, clad in black.

"I remember this," Santiago kept saying. "I remember this."

It dawned on the miner that the look in the demon's eyes was not surprise but recognition, and that he clenched his fist with fury, not fear. Years ago and in another body, he must have stood there in the trees, as he did then, and watched himself reduced to ashes simply, impossibly, by reaching for the fetus of the miner's child. He wrapped his fingers around the front of the miner's shirt and pulled him close, skin sizzling into vapor.

"Again and again," Santiago whispered, "no matter how many times I try, I always return to this moment when I felt death for the first time. I don't remember the first time I stood in those woods. Look at me." The miner looked at Santiago sprawled beneath him. "No," the demon said, eyeing the aspen. "Look at *me*. I am terrified." The miner faced the woods. The bulky figure turned and barged deep into the aspen, felling trees with heavy, cracking footsteps. "I was so terrified of my fate, but my frustration grew. I went after your boy. I went after your wife. I went after you. And your fathers, and your fathers' fathers—"

The miner peeled Santiago's fingers from his shirt. "Tell me how to operate the suit. Tell me how to get us back."

Santiago stared into the vacant woods, unfazed. "I tried everything. Finally I said fuck it, and I took your wife and

I brought her here to murder your boy before your eyes. It would be different this time. But it was not." Vapor buried the demon's body, white and humid. He was emaciated. "I will wake up soon in another body and I will do the whole fucking thing over again, even though I know it will end me. I cannot help myself. And there is no devil to blame for leading me astray other than the bastard before you..."

He smiled, but his eyes glistened. The miner turned Santiago's head away from the aspen. "I need to get her back—"

"Time travel is infuriating," the demon persisted. "It is like losing your balance underwater, not knowing up or down. You hold your breath and swim in whatever fucking direction and hope you don't drown." He pressed his fingers against his face and swallowed. "Every time, I know it will end me. I still don't understand how. But I want so badly to make your boy feel what I do now. He should feel life zipping out of him. That little shit should know what it's like to drown ... I want so bad ... You could not imagine."

The miner shook the demon. His body was impossibly light but hot, burning into vapor. He was mostly vapor now. "Show me how to work the damn machine."

"Why?" the vapor whispered.

His wife shivered in the suit and began to scream quietly. The black metal coughed. The miner panted into the vapor, fists and knees planted against the shrouded earth.

"Because you know how this will end."

The demon parted his translucent lips and stared again into the aspen. He placed the palm of his right hand atop his chest and wheezed. His tongue moved as he tried to speak, emitting a dry sound. He looked back at the miner, closed his eyes, and nodded.

"Thank you." The miner bowed his head.

He lifted Santiago so he leaned over the suit, and the demon reached into the metal. A drooping finger brushed the suit's thigh, where the metal had ruptured. *Broken,* came the implication. *It can't walk.* The same finger pointed into the black sky. *But can travel.* Mustache twitching, he released a gauge in the suit and nodded. The miner began to let him down, but the demon's body collapsed into vapor. Santiago slipped like searing white sand between his fingers.

Inside the suit, machinery whirred and gears spun. The miner heard the erratic sound of electricity and the drum of clockwork. He kissed his wife once more and closed the metal over her shivering body. The suit barked and vibrated. It contracted, became thinner than a blade of grass, and whisked into the light of the aspen's flame.

"Our child killed the Devil," the miner confessed to Tomás. "We were nervous about the child. She was having night terrors. She would scream during her sleep. But her belly had yet to show signs of it. Our child was the seed of a living thing, but still it killed him. Santiago was ended by a seed. I feel bad for the fellow. That's a pathetic way to die, to be killed by a thing not yet born. That is why he is so afraid of time."

Tomás gripped his own arm and rubbed the hair from his skin. "Milagros," he whispered.

The miner wiped his eyes. "I don't believe I mentioned her name."

Tomás blinked. "It i-is my mother's."

As Uncle Tomás recounts this to me, I see the realization grow in him as it did then for his father. It's as if he is processing for the first time the shock of the revelation. As if, in articulating this piece of their history, it's become real. I watch his pupils contract and glow as the traffic light overhead turns green. His cigarette hangs loose between his index and middle fingers and teeters in the breeze.

I understand now my abuelos' attention to discipline. Neither had known any place other than their homeland, and then here they were in Manhattan, where they could not speak the language or breathe fresh air or dip their feet into warm, clean water and hot white sand. It was a place as obscure and terrifying as Santiago's primordial lair, propelled impossibly by itself. Surely such a thing could not last. Where did their children go when they went to school or work? Who did they speak to, and what did they speak about? Did Santiago lurk in these streets as he did in the waters and mountains of their homeland, in the loins of Trujillo and his men, in their forts and convoys? If their children misbehaved, would they slip into a crevice, deep as the rift of the Sierra de Bahoruco, from which there was no escape? Their children did stupid things.

And Mom's words, both a warning and prideful declaration. *Kicked out of every place we go.* Maybe this is what my abuelos feared. Maybe this is why Mom says things like that.

Uncle Tomás opens and closes his mouth. "Your grandfather and me, we just sorta stood there. Staring."

Tomás struggled to calm his breathing. He pretended he was dipping in and out of the Dominican surf, and he allowed the sound of the aspen's flame to consume him like the unending noise of breaking waves. Abuelo's lips flattened and pursed. With one finger he touched the thick rim of his spectacles.

"What will we call you?"

"Rafael Tomás Paoli."

They reached forward with hesitation. Abuelo sandwiched Tomás's right hand between both of his. "It is nice to meet you, Rafael Tomás Paoli." He chuckled. "She had to have her way, didn't she ... I would have preferred—oh, I should not say. That would confuse you. You are already so confused. It is a great pleasure to meet you, my son."

He continued to grip Tomás's hand. His skin was callused and warm.

They strode to an adjacent hill and watched as the flame inched across the trembling aspen. In its wake, wisps of gray and black rose into the ether. The forest extended beyond the limits of their sight.

Abuelo explained that Santiago had referred to this land as a place outside of space and time, a sanctuary from which no action originated and no action followed. The Devil was a hive mind, Abuelo said. He was like the trembling aspen. He was one and he was many. He burned continually by his own perpetuation. "We can pity this Santiago," he said, "but another will come, and another and another, always searching to impregnate our line with his own. He wants a future as much as we do. Time is infinitely malleable to him, but it binds him also. He knows death, even if he will be reborn in another body in another suit of armor."

He placed an arm around Tomás, who stiffened and avoided his gaze.

"Tell me about yourself." He winked. "You are a man now. We've skipped the pain of getting there, haven't we? That is to come for me if I get out of here. Tell me, Tomás. Do you have anyone?"

Tomás opened his mouth and closed it. He stared at the distant flame and watched the shadows along the floor of the aspen forest. They danced as the fire flickered in slow, broad gestures of red and yellow. He opened his mouth again when the wind buzzed.

I got no one.

The grass trembled beneath the weight of a heavy step. The stench of gasoline filled his throat. Tomás twisted out of Abuelo's embrace as Santiago strode from the rear of the hill. It was the younger Santiago, the one who had fled into the aspen days ago. The light of the aspen's flame struck the black metal, revealing its many parts and filling each dent and scratch with furious color. The glare burned his eyes. He shielded his brow and glimpsed two men reflected off a shard along the demon's shin. They looked like the same man.

Tomás stood.

"Good!" he shouted. He pressed a fist against his chest. "Santiago, let's finish this. I finished you once. I'll finish you again."

Abuelo looked between the two, stumbling over his words as the demon approached. "I am sure we can reach a reasonable—"

"You cannot fight me, boy," the demon bellowed.

"I c-can fight you. I c-can take you out. I did it once. I can do it again."

"You fool. You think I still will not kill you. You forget where you are. This land is beyond space, beyond time, beyond law, beyond right and wrong. Here, my actions have no consequences."

Tomás scowled and craned his neck to look him in the eye.

"But I, uh, killed you over there." He pointed. "I wasn't even fucking born and I killed you. It got consequences."

The demon teetered his weight from one foot to the other.

His eyes darted across the landscape. His expression loosened, and his lower lip quivered.

Abuelo stepped forward.

"I am sure there is some equitable solution—"

The demon laughed, ignoring Abuelo's pleas. "God thinks It has made a lesson for me out of your kind. God thinks It has demonstrated the value of your kind. But God is wrong. I'll show God."

As the demon spoke, Tomás tiptoed between his legs. He positioned himself behind the demon.

"I'll show It my own lesson. I'll show God you are nothing more than clay."

Tomás leapt onto the demon's back, clutched a protrusion of metal with both hands, pressed the soles of his shoes against the suit, and yanked. The metal was coarse, blunt along the edges, and cool. The demon screamed and writhed, but Tomás would not relinquish his grip.

"I got him in a death hold," Uncle Tomás tells me, "and I pulled and I pulled and then finally—*phoosh!* The back of the suit went flying!"

Tomás and the demon fell. Santiago panted on all fours, while Tomás rebounded and tore the demon from the cavity he'd wrenched along the spine of the suit. He lifted a dislodged shard of armor hidden in the grass and raised it above his head. Santiago cowered beneath him, mustache in disarray and skin lacerated and blistered by the marks of the suit. Abuelo was running toward him, shouting, but Tomás could hear nothing except the roar of the trembling aspen's primordial flame, rushing and incessant, as he struck downward with the strength of his mighty breaststroke. There was a loud crunch. Santiago gasped. The demon's skin sizzled; zits developed and popped as it boiled. Sinews of gas rose from the stinking pus and spiraled into the darkness overhead.

Abuelo reached Tomás and leaned wheezing against the suit.

"Tomás," he hissed. "What son have I raised? What curse are you upon yourself? It means nothing to kill him. I told you as much. The Devil is a hive mind. This is merely a body to him. I feared he would impregnate our family, but it appears he already has."

Tomás scowled. "I don't wanna hear it. You're just a fucking coal miner—"

"Bauxite," Abuelo retorted. "I mine bauxite. Our future is bauxite, Tomás, from cans to rockets. Imagine a world without metal. We are cavemen without it—"

He looked down upon Santiago's bleeding and burning carcass. His skin grew pale.

"Oh God," Abuelo murmured. "So much blood…"

His eyes rolled into their sockets, and his body fell limp into the grass. He sprawled in the shining blades of green while a line of drool crept from the corner of his mouth. He was still breathing.

On Amsterdam, Uncle Tomás stamps on his cigarette.

"Told you your Abuelo was like that. He couldn't take the sight of blood."

"So what did you do?" I ask.

"I dug my way back to Barahona."

When only vapor remained of Santiago's body, Tomás climbed into the chasm of the suit and allowed it to assemble around him. Inside, it was dark and cold, and he could smell his sweat and feel the demon's blood lubricate the boundary between his skin and the iron lining. He nestled in the darkness and closed his eyes.

He rose after a moment. Dirt and rock slid from the armor. He kneeled, raised Abuelo from the grass, and wandered deep into the trembling aspen in search of the collapsed rock his father had mined. When he found it hours later, Tomás placed Abuelo on the ground and approached the cave. He pulled rocks from the rubble and, once he'd established an opening, pummeled through the buildup. He dove into the earth, burrowing through excavated rock without pain or effort. He realized now why the demon was so thin and weak when he was out of his suit. The suit provided all of his strength. Tomás tore through the earth, sending red soil into the air. I imagine the particles of soil as they are, relics from the Miocene churned into a tornado of red mist, dry and ancient as the throat of Shai-hulud, a colossal worm buried in the sands of Frank Herbert's desert planet, Dune. Shai-hulud is the incarnation of God in the world, to earth what Christ is to man. Shai-hulud, eternal and material, godlike and feared, worshipped and demonized.

Hours later, Tomás broke through the loose earth into a cavern perched on the bank of the Ozama River.

"I knew the place because I'd been there before," Uncle Tomás tells me. "It's under that old church where Carlos and Mike and me used to swim."

Through the stained-glass visor, the cavern rock appeared blue and green. He punched open the visor and the world became yellow. The air reeked of mud. Mayflies danced over the surface of the water, and sunlight poured from the cavities in the cavern walls. He walked back through the cave, retrieved Abuelo, and laid him on a smooth slab of rock. His spectacles blinded Tomás with reflected light.

"Bye, Papá."

Tomás stared down his neck to the dials beneath his

breastplate. "It was a time machine like your abuelo said," he explains to me, eyes big. "I was coming back. Like Arnold Schwarzenegger."

"You knew how to work that thing?" I ask. He can barely put together a cabinet.

Uncle Tomás shrugs. "I dunno. I tried for a while, but the thing was a fucking rocket ship, boy. And then it ... worked." He pauses and reaches for his pack of cigarettes, but there are none left. I watch him fiddle with his thick yellow nails. "I was very sad, Jihad. I missed home a lot. I sat there for a while and I, uh ..."

"Yeah?"

"I was very sad," he repeated. "I thought about your mother. And then all of a sudden the suit started shaking. What the fuck! My whole body went crazy like a seizure or some shit like that, and the visor went smashing down and the suit got so fucking *hot*—"

His body whirred into motion. He escaped through the sunlight and seconds later plunged into Riverside Park. Half the suit had lodged into the ground so that he stuck out at an oblique angle. A fine layer of white covered the earth. The moan of New York City tumbled leisurely through the air. Thick snow drifted from the sky.

Tomás wrenched himself from the mud and ice and grinned.

Outside the campus gates, Uncle Tomás tosses his empty pack into the trash bin.

"That's how it happened," he concludes, rubbing his eyes. "That's how I fucking killed the Devil."

"You didn't kill the Devil," I protest.

"Sure I did!"

"You killed *a* devil."

"Hey," Uncle Tomás warns, "next time you pull that shit off you call me, all right?" He smirks and pinches my arm. "You fuck."

I raise my eyebrows. "Maybe I will."

✳

I'm in Stamford, Connecticut, waiting for the train to campus when I overhear an old white woman talking to a middle-aged black woman a few feet away. ". . . and that's how you say it in German," the old woman is telling the other. "I am from Germany." She has had plastic surgery, and her loose but kempt hair is bleached dark blond. She wears crimson lipstick. Her jacket and purse are dark yellow. They appear gold, but upon further inspection I'm pretty sure they're knockoffs. Her suitcase is green and blue.

I sit, engrossed in my book. I am taking a course on jihad and the modern state. My professor is preoccupied by Foucault. He describes him as a thoroughgoing Ghazalian and relates Foucault's technologies of the self to Al-Ghazali's. Foucault's technologies are those of the state: the mechanisms of culture and law that shape the citizen. The believer without ritual exposes herself to this machinery, for ritual embodies Al-Ghazali's technologies. It supplements the jihad of the soul, the struggle to improve the self. In the previous seminar, my professor asked us where struggle begins. "Does it begin with the lesser jihad, the struggle against the material enemy—the social, the legal, the political? Or does it begin with the greater jihad, the struggle against the enemy within oneself?" I raised my hand and expressed dissatisfaction with the question.

"From the believer's point of view, the Devil is the ultimate enemy. He is *the* enemy," I said. I paraphrased the last lines of the fourth Qul, the final chapter of the Qur'an. "It says, you know, protect us from the whispers of the Devil, who whispers into the hearts of men and jinn. So the Devil comes from outside—the enemy without—but he enters through the heart—from within." I closed my fingers into the shape of a beak and bore into my chest. "So what does it mean to say there's an internal and an external struggle when the ultimate enemy, the Devil himself, operates with both? I don't think we can really say there is a divided internal and external." I weaved my fingers together. "They create each other. They're, you know, intertwined."

I looked at my professor. He nodded, eyes twinkling.

"Yes, Jihad," he exclaimed, "but if we say everything creates everything, then how the hell are we supposed to understand anything? We will be left without definition."

At the train station, I'm reading Iqbal. He's obsessed with free will and a saying of the Prophet Muhammad: "Do not vilify time, for time is God." I still don't get it. I think about Abuelo's last words to Uncle Tomás, and I try to understand how my uncle's fetus could kill Santiago. It might have to do with Abuelo and the jungle he decimated in Barahona, the underwater mountains of the Sierra de Bahoruco nestled along the DR's tectonic ridge, the ancient power the bauxite mines awakened from the Miocene like Shai-hulud lured from crests of sand by the steady beat of a Fremen thumper. But Santiago's history. And Abuelo's equivocal admission. *I feared he would impregnate our family, but it appears he already has.* The fetus killed Santiago because Santiago could not kill Tomás. As Santiago was our ancestor, he would also become our successor. To kill Tomás would be to sever his own ancestral line, and therefore himself. The act would erase his past and future alike. God—the jungle, Sierra de Bahoruco, and the bauxite—had, in an aversion to paradox, prevented Santiago from doing so.

I close my book and hold it with either palm between my knees. From whose loins will Santiago enter this world, only for him to fall backward through time, through New York, the DR, New York again, Italy, and finally Corsica, so that he kneels before General Pasquale Paoli and offers him his sword? Will he know the monster he will have become, that he has already become? I know now Abuelo's pity.

Beside me, this guy is rocking back and forth in his seat like he's doing dhikr. He's wrapped a gray hoodie over his head. He keeps screaming, "Heavy metal! Heavy metal!" into the open platform. Travelers stride by quickly and at a distance. He has a foreign accent. It sounds like he's high. It's hard to get a look at his face, but I see that his skin is dark and his nails are dry.

The old woman approaches.

"Hello," she says. "May I sit here?"

He looks up. "Yes, do you like heavy metal?"

She sits down and clutches the handle of her suitcase. "Tell me," she asks, oblivious to his question, "are you Arabic?"

"I like heavy metal!" he shouts, as if answering himself. He laughs.

She persists. "Tell me, where were you born?" she asks.

"I am from . . ." The man is quiet. He rocks back and forth. "I am from here."

"Where?" she replies, almost surprised.

"Here," he repeats. "Stam. Ford."

"Your family is from here?"

"Yes, yes," he answers hurriedly.

"Where were you born? Were you born here? I can hear

Russian," she says in a way that makes me wonder if she's racist, as if she can't understand that a man with an accent can come from the States.

"I was born … in many places."

"Ah," she says. "You have had a few too many drinks, have you? I can smell it on you."

"Yes, yes," he says. "With Veronica last night. It was very nice."

"Ah, that was nice?"

"Yes, very nice." He nods and continues rocking. He mumbles to himself and then, loudly: "Where are you from?"

"I am from Germany. I was born in Germany. I am German. But I live in New York." She presses again. "How about you?"

He nods. "Yes, I am from Ukraine."

"Ah," she says, satisfied at last with an answer. "That makes sense."

"Where are you going?" he asks.

"I am going to New York."

"But you are from…" He pauses. "You are from Germany?"

"I am from Germany, but I live in New York now."

He nods and says with confidence, "I am from Ukraine."

She nods also. "Yes, I am from Germany," she says with equal certitude, as if he's conveyed impressed disbelief about the fact. "My father died in Ukraine in the war, you know, but that was a long time ago."

"Yes, heavy metal! Ha ha."

"It was a long time ago now." The old woman stands and pats her suitcase. "Well, I am going to leave this here now. I am just going to leave this here, okay? I am going to come back in a moment. One moment. Okay."

He doesn't respond, but she doesn't seem to notice. She

leaves the suitcase and walks to the Dunkin' Donuts. The Ukrainian guy sits there rocking. He stinks.

"I am Ukrainian, yes. Ha ha! Heavy metal. Heavy metal!" He is quiet for a minute. Abruptly, he stands and walks in a straight line toward the station exit, light-gray hoodie wrapped tightly around him, arms in his kangaroo pocket like he's in a straitjacket. The woman returns and sits, then faces somewhere ahead of her and to her right. She raises her voice and speaks emphatically to the empty space: "You two, you enjoy now."

I realize she is as crazy as the Ukrainian.

A middle-aged woman walks by a minute later and sits down in the Ukrainian's place. She is wearing a puffy red fleece and has slung a black handbag around her shoulder. Her hair is tied. The old woman turns to her.

"Hello. I am German. I am from Germany, but I am going to New York. My father died in Ukraine, you know. But I am from Germany, you see…"

I scratch my chin and stare into the station exit. The Ukrainian is zigzagging through the parking lot. I grab my backpack and jacket and weave through the crowd. An officer watches me from outside the concession stand, an unopened pack of Marlboro Reds between his fingers, a tabloid in his armpit, and a palm against his holstered baton. I notice a young woman in front of me. Her head is inclined toward the train schedule and a camera slung around her neck. She is familiar. The freckles around her nose, the curls behind her ears, the way the skin along her neck wrinkles as she gazes upward—GRAND CENTRAL. NEW HAVEN. BRIDGEPORT.—her hips, the dark red tank top. "Glory?" I say, but as she turns toward me I see that her eyes are the wrong shade of gray.

They are too dark. I blink and push past her into the parking lot.

The lot is vacant. The air buzzes. I meander to the lowest level. I hear footsteps behind me, but the Ukrainian is nowhere. The buzzing is louder. I can hear the sound of moving parts. This is not a steady sound like the trains overhead. It is erratic. I toss my bag and jacket onto the asphalt and follow the buzzing. The noise seeps in through my small ear, and I track it to a pillar on my right. My blood roars as I feel the surface. It is cold, and I can smell Windex. The footsteps are louder. I jerk my head around. I am alone.

"Hello?" I say.

I know Santiago is here. I can hear him moving along the edges of everything, in the corners and along the cracks in the cement. I will force him from his hiding place, I decide. *I'm finished hiding. I'm finished waiting.*

I move my lips to reply, but I realize the words are my own. They pour down from the wires overhead and the crevices in the asphalt, but they sound like an echo. It is as if I have just heard these words, as if they've already been said.

I hear something click on the asphalt. I turn. The young woman from the platform is striding toward me from a distance.

It's about time.

I search. Through my small ear, I can feel him move. He's shifting quickly from one pillar to another, across the walls and over the outlines of vehicles. He's enraged, terrified, faster than anything I've ever known. His movements are piecewise, jumping from one place to the next. For a second he is nowhere. A moment later he is in the pillar beside me, rushing down something buried in the cement.

The young woman is closer.

"I don't know you," I call out. "I'm sorry about before. I didn't mean anything."

She keeps walking, backpack slung over one shoulder, flip-flops slapping against her bare heels. She looks ridiculous surrounded by cement and vehicles. She belongs on a beach, where there are waves and trees and sand, where the sun shines and the breeze is warm and salt is in our noses and we can know the sea is close before we see it.

She lifts the camera to her left eye and begins to turn the focus.

"I don't know you," I insist.

I turn away, ball my fingers into a fist, and swing at the pillar. The movement is involuntary, and as I follow through I close my eyes and grit my teeth. But I feel no pain. I open my eyes. The cement has shattered into gray and brown detritus, and behind the structure a bundle of wires flows to the ceiling. My fist is unscathed. My bones vibrate like thick cable. The wires blink and flicker, and I wrestle them free. Sparks fly and light fills the basement level of the parking lot.

I wait for something to step from the light, but the space before me is vacant. I rub my eyes as the flash dissipates in my retinas. Loose detritus tumbles from the pillar. I notice the footsteps are gone. I turn back.

The young woman has stopped about fifteen cars behind me. She drops her backpack and kicks off her flip-flops. For a moment her eyes are the right shade of gray, clearer. I begin to smile. But she brings the camera between us again and closes the distance. As she passes below the lights her shoulders grow broader, her feet thicker, her footsteps heavy. Black modules climb from the camera. They assemble outward, and the pieces envelop her body. She hunkers beneath the ceiling, black metal spine dusting the cement overhead, iron-gloved fingers marking the asphalt. The suit fills the space, humming, intricate, colossal.

The figure punches open its visor. I recognize the red mustache and blue eyes. I recognize Uncle Tomás's charcoal breath. A grin carves a slender mark across pasty cheeks.

"Pleased to meet you," Santiago sneers. And then, with quiet fury: "Joe."

I reach into my pocket and grip my prayer beads. I clench the muscles in my gut as if this will steady my heart, and I tune out the sound of blood in my eardrums. I step closer, matching his gaze with mine.

"That's not my name."

CREDITS

Author	Haris A. Durrani
First Readers	Jennifer Boylan, Sauleha Kamal, Armando Lozano, Chris Owen, Aneem Talukder, and Adam Wilson
Copyeditor	Kelly Lauer
Cover Art	Mary Mazziotti
Cover Design	Ranita Haanen
Proofreader	Annamarie Bellegante
Interior Design	Williams Writing, Editing & Design

AUTHOR'S ACKNOWLEDGMENTS

I feel obliged to cite the preface of Karen Barad's *Meeting the Universe Halfway*: "The past is never finished. It cannot be wrapped up like a package, or a scrapbook, or an acknowledgment." Thus, my thanks here must inevitably remain incomplete. I am grateful first to Michael Fulton, my Yoda, Gandalf, Dumbledore, and Spock, without whom none of my work, let alone this book, would have reached the world. Ruthie Knox and Mary Ann Rivers for supporting this story and its vision. Maxine Vande Vaarst for believing in its protagonist. Jennifer Boylan for nurturing the book from its seedling beginnings with honesty. Adam Wilson for his counsel and his confidence in the early drafts. My peers in Advanced Projects in Prose at Barnard and Advanced Fiction at Columbia for their thoughtful criticism, without which this book would surely be a lesser animal. My loyal first readers—Sauleha Kamal, Armando Lozano, Chris Owen, and Aneem Talukder—for their careful, necessary feedback. Hisham Matar for teaching me the value of patience in the craft. James Hannaham for his sharp guidance and kind support. John Crowley for believing wholeheartedly in my work and championing my growth as a writer. John Joseph Adams for showing me my first glimpses of the publishing world. Beth Harrison, Anan Barqawi, Seth Dickinson, Diane Turnshek, and Usman Malik for their advice. The Alpha Science Fiction/Fantasy/Horror Workshop for Young Writers for providing the first steps of my writing career. The staff, old and new, of the Alliance for Young Artists and Writers for supporting my writing since my first Gold

Key. Hammaad Chaudry for his ever-articulate advice on negotiating the writer's world. Taimur Malik for encouraging me to attend the Yale Writers' Conference. Priom Ahmed, Hamdan Azhar, Sameea Butt, Anelise Chen, Shezza Dallal, Habiba Khokhar, Jyothi Natarajan, Bushra Rehman, Zainab Shah, Alay Syed, Mirzya Syed, Ryan Tyler, Will Waller, and Hamna Zubair for their warm reception of my earlier work. The friends, community members, and writers who made the Muslim Protagonist Symposium possible for challenging my assumptions and for showing me these stories are worth writing. The Muslim Writers Collective, the Unpublished Reading Series, and the Asian American Writers' Workshop for their support. I am especially grateful to my extended family; if I write with love, it is only because they provided it. Most importantly, these pages would remain blank if it were not for my parents' inviolable love and their unwavering support for my writing. This places me among a lucky few. And, of course, Uncle Tomás.

This book owes its title, theme, and impetus to Wael Hallaq's characterization of Foucault as "a thoroughgoing Ghazalian" in *The Impossible State*. I must thank him for his epistemic jihad and for passionately teaching me to seek out the straight path to water.

Brain Mill Press would like to acknowledge the support of the following Patrons:

Noelle Adams

Rhyll Biest

Katherine Bodsworth

Lea Franczak

Barry and Barbara Homrighaus

Kelly Lauer

Susan Lee

Sherri Marx

Aisling Murphy

Audra North

Molly O'Keefe

Virginia Parker

Cherri Porter

Erin Rathjen

Robin Drouin Tuch

ABOUT THE AUTHOR

Photo courtesy Ana Espinola, *The Eye,* Columbia University

Haris A. Durrani is an M.Phil. candidate in History and Philosophy of Science at the University of Cambridge. He holds a B.S. in Applied Physics from Columbia University, where he minored in Middle Eastern, South Asian, and African Studies and cofounded the Muslim Protagonist Symposium. His work has appeared in *Comparative Islamic Studies, Buffalo Almanack, Analog Science Fiction and Fact, The New York Review of Science Fiction, Media Diversified, altMuslimah,* and *The Best Teen Writing of 2012* (editor), *2011,* and *2010.* He is an alum of the Alpha Science Fiction/Fantasy/Horror Workshop for Young Writers and was a 2011 Portfolio Gold Medalist in the Scholastic Art and Writing Awards, for which he currently serves on the Alumni Council. He will enroll at Columbia Law School in fall 2016. When he grows up, he would like to live on Gliese 581 g, if it exists.

CPSIA information can be obtained
at www.ICGtesting.com
Printed in the USA
FSOW01n0521290216
17283FS